for love I will

Library of Congress Cataloging-in-Publication Data
Sterling, C.D.
Title: For Love I Will: a novel / C.D. Sterling
Description: First Edition
Identifiers: LCCN 2024914546
ISBN: 979-8-9911366-1-7 (paperback)
ISBN: 979-8-9911366-2-4 (hardcover)
ISBN: 979-8-9911366-0-0 (ebook)

C.D. Sterling

for love I will

A NOVEL

Unify Writers

TEXAS

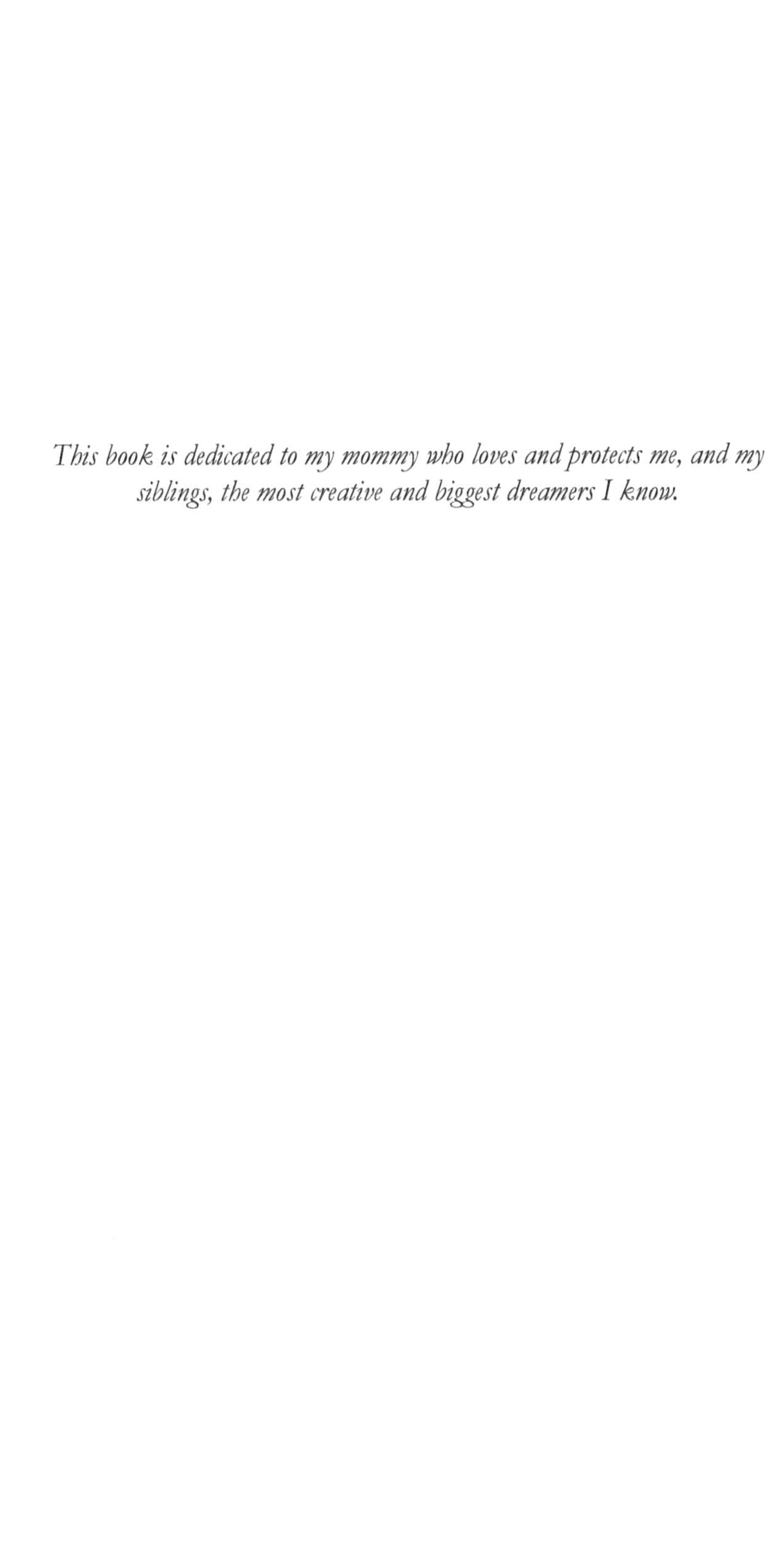

This book is dedicated to my mommy who loves and protects me, and my siblings, the most creative and biggest dreamers I know.

AUTHOR'S NOTE

Hi reader, I'm C.D. Sterling. Thank you for giving this story a chance. I wrote this story for people torn between what the mind wants and what the heart needs. It contains mental health and LGBTQIA+ characters.

This story was developed based on a question I once asked myself, how to choose between the love I want or need? Over time, I've learned love is a deep affection with moments and memories. It's powerful but it's also respect.

Writing has been a passion of mine since I was fourteen. Thank you for your time and I look forward to hearing from you.

HELLO RILEY
Friday

I'm looking forward to the new year—living in a different city, starting a new life, and making new friends. Rochester has been fantastic so far. At least, that's what I'm telling myself. Fascinating, right? I'm twenty-two with freckles, six feet tall, have light brown skin, am average weight, and by average, I mean I have a belly—nothing too big though. Let us not forget the short brown curly hairdo. I'm not a gorgeous person, but I am attractive. Also, I work as an EMT, and on my off-time, I indulge in binge-watching television.

It's a day off for me and I'm at my local frozen yogurt place, minding my own business. I look to my right and see one of the most beautiful women. I've noticed her before. She's gorgeous, with hazel eyes, caramel skin, light brown curly hair, and stands about 5'8". Then I realize that she's walking closer and her eyes are staring straight into mine. My heart begins to race and I look down—maybe she didn't notice me looking at her first.

After getting my order, I do my best to appear casual while walking over to the nearest table I can find. I sit down and immediately take a bite of my mango-flavored frozen yogurt.

"Treat," is what I hear when she talks to me.

"Excuse me?" is what I manage to say.

"So, I've been wondering; do you always treat yourself to the same flavor?" she asks with a smirk.

"I do, it's very satisfying." Ugh, what was I thinking? Maybe I should have said something more relaxed. Nonetheless, she is still standing here. Focus, Cameron.

"Why not try the others? I'm sure some are just as satisfying as mango," she responds while tucking a curl behind her ear.

What made her approach me? It's not just because of frozen yogurt, right?

"I'll take that into consideration the next time I get some," I say with a laugh.

"What's your deal?" She pulls out a chair and eats a spoonful of her yogurt.

"Deal?"

A grin appears on her lips. "Yeah, I've noticed you come here often, and each time I also notice you watching me."

What??? Oh no, could this get more embarrassing? "I…"

"Let me take a guess. Either you're obsessed with frozen yogurt or you're into me."

She laughs as she scoops another spoonful of yogurt into her mouth. I mean I am aware that she comes here, and each time it's hard not to look at her. And now she's talking to me. Her voice is calming, and her laugh is a beautiful thing to hear. It might sound weird, but there's just something about this girl I can't quite put my finger on.

"Well…I…you see."

"You're cute," she says.

My jaw drops at those words. A beautiful woman sitting across from me, who could most likely get any guy she wants, just called me "cute."

"Thank you," I try to say while stuffing my mouth.

"What are you doing tomorrow?"

Is this girl asking me out? I should be asking *her* out. She's beautiful. And who would have thought a yellow and grey plaid shirt with white shorts would look so good on someone?

"Nothing planned."

"Well let's change that."

What!!!

"Uhhhh, sure, what do you have in mind?" I ask.

"Hmmmm." She leans back in the chair as she collects her thoughts.

There are so many things we could do, but in this moment, my brain sort of stalls and there's only one thing I can think of.

"How about a nightclub?" I suggest.

"Sounds like fun. I'm Riley, by the way," she says, holding out her hand.

Wow, no nail polish. I guess she's not into that.

"I'm Cameron; nice to meet you." As I grab her hand to shake it, I notice how beautiful her smile is up close.

"So, where exactly is this club?"

"It's on the east side of town, maybe fifteen minutes from here." I shift and hit my knee on the table. I tend to bang up against things when I am nervous or in a rush.

"Did that hurt?" she asks.

"No, I'm okay; I probably should've sat at a higher table."

She smiles again. "So what time are we meeting? By the way, I like your shirt; it's very posh."

I look down at the ombre-colored shirt I have on with fitted blue jean shorts, cropped above the knee. "Oh, thanks. I just moved into a new place and still have to unpack."

She stares and keeps smiling.

"I grabbed the first shirt I saw." Good to know she likes my choice of clothing.

"Well, I'm getting ready to head out. Would you like to exchange contact info?" she asks while pulling out her phone.

"I'd like that," I say while grinning back at her. She reaches for my phone and starts typing. I do the same once she hands me hers.

"So just let me know what time to pick you up."

Wow, beautiful and confident.

"Wouldn't it be better if I picked you up?" I challenge her.

"It would be nice; however, I think it would be better if I did the picking up; after all, I approached you." She places a strand of hair behind her left ear and I laugh.

"Okay Riley, how does 7 o'clock tomorrow night sound?" "That's okay with me," she says, putting a finger to her chin. I hand back her phone and she returns mine.

"Okay, I'll see you tomorrow night," I reply.

HELLO LEAH

"Wait, she did what?" my best friend Leah asks with a smirk.

She came over as soon as I told her.

"Maybe I should be more spontaneous and walk up to a guy and say, 'Hey, you're sexy, so am I; let's go out.'"

I sit there as she flips her hair, trying to contain my laughter.

"She didn't say I was sexy; she just said she liked my shirt," I explain.

"Cameron, being naïve is not a good look on you. It's obvious she was into you; otherwise she would've stayed where she was standing casually, and left."

She has a sip of the green mint tea with honey I brewed minutes before she arrived. It's something new I am trying; usually, I would get some pre-made sweet tea somewhere with ice. I figured making my own with honey instead of sugar might be a healthier option.

"Well, I'm not quite sure what to make of it, but just glad it happened," I respond.

She rolls her eyes.

"Enough about my day; let's talk about you for the moment. How are things at work?"

She stands up and begins to rant. "My boss is the most inconsiderate human being ever; I mean, who tells someone they have to cover two shifts after it's been explained to them that there aren't any last-minute caretakers available in the Rochester metro area?"

Leah's mom has been pretty ill for the past two weeks. She says she is coping with it and fine, but I can't help sense that she's hurting and does not want to admit it.

"I can watch her after I get off," I offer. I have volunteered to help her on multiple occasions, but she always refuses.

"No, I'll figure something out."

I walk towards the kitchen to fix another cup of tea, and she follows.

"I'm sorry, I know you want to help, Cameron, and I thank you for that, but I want to do this on my own," she says emphatically.

"I'm here whenever you need anything, and I don't want you to feel you can't come to me; you're my best friend, and I care about you," I say and hug her.

"Thank you love, but you're not getting out of this taking charge of some female action," she says, laughing.

"I want to meet her. When is this date happening?" She grins from ear to ear.

"It's tomorrow at 7 PM; I'm not even sure it's a date; it's more of a get-together between two people who seem to like each other," I assure her.

She scoffs and glares at me while folding her arms.

"Yeah, okay. I'm not sure if you even believe that."

"And what do you believe it is?" I stare at her waiting for her to explain how she thinks I feel.

"Okay, let's look at the facts: she approaches you, creates small talk, compliments your choice of clothing, suggests your next meeting, exchanges numbers with you, and says she'll pick you up. My friend that is a date."

"Well, since you're such an expert, then tell me what you think I should wear?"

She rolls her eyes at my question. "It's obvious we have to go shopping. No offense, but your wardrobe could use some updating."

I laugh. It's true I could use some color. Most of my clothing is either black or grey; it wouldn't hurt to brighten things up a bit.

"Fine, when do we do this?" I lean back into the sofa.

"Now. Tomorrow's your date and we're going to need all the time we can get."

Of course we do. This particular activity with Leah is exhausting. Not only does it take a while for her to shop, but it takes even longer when we shop for me. We once spent four hours looking for one pair of shoes.

"Leah, I don't want to spend all day in a store. Can't we just find something here?"

"Cam, sweetheart, this is a date. New attire is appropriate for the occasion."

Says who? There are clothes in my closet with the tags still on that have yet to be worn. I'm not sure why I even bother to ask; there will always be a debate with her. Whether it's clothes, food, or even a vacation, she will find an argument, or in her words, "It's just a discussion, Cam."

"What about the black polo button-up shirt I bought three months ago?"

"It's spring now; we need something brighter."

Ugh. I turn on my back and look up at the ceiling. It's been a while since I've been on a date, but I didn't expect preparing for one would be so draining.

"Cam! Get up," she shouts.

No, just let me lie here in peace. Leah storms over and pulls me off the couch. I almost fall on my face.

"Let's go."

And now the real torture begins.

HELLO REECE

"What about this one? I think this would go great with your skin tone." She picks up a maroon crewneck shirt.

"You don't think it's too plain?"

Maybe I should've gone shopping alone.

"Plain? Well, now look who's got an opinion about clothing now."

I roll my eyes. "All I'm saying is, if it is a date, I want her to look at me and see that I put some effort and thought into what I'm wearing." I continue searching through racks.

"Um, first, it is definitely a date, and second, you're going to a nightclub, not just a restaurant. Third, I consider shopping for new clothing to be very thoughtful; you could've easily worn something old."

She does have valid points, but I still want to try.

"What about this?" I show her a V-neck turquoise sweater, which is not too heavy.

"Okay, not bad; I like that. Now let's look for bottoms."

"I think a pair of jeans would be nice with that."

"Of course, you would, Cam, but there are options other than jeans."

"What's wrong with jeans, Leah?"

She sighs and looks at me with her eyes ready to attack.

"Nothing is wrong with jeans; however, you have many pairs already."

"Yeah but…"

Leah walks to the far left of the store. Ugh, so annoying. I might as well continue looking at tops. As I turn to check out the rack behind me, I bump into someone who's the same height as me. But that's where the similarities stop; you could tell that he works out a lot and he has ginger hair with pale skin. Wow, are his eyes actually grey? Either way, his looks are a little intimidating; I probably should get a gym membership.

"My apologies, I didn't see you," I say with a laugh.

"No worries," he says, returning my grin.

Is that an accent I'm detecting?

"I should just pay more attention to my surroundings." I laugh nervously.

"I'm Reece, and you are?" He extends his hand.

"I'm Cameron. Nice to make your acquaintance."

Oh no, I cannot believe I just said, "Make your acquaintance."

"Are you from here, Cameron?" he questions.

"I'm from Texas originally, but moved to New York for a fresh start."

He raises a brow. "Fresh start? Might I ask why? My apologies if that's too invasive." I hesitate for a moment.

"I'm twenty-two years old and realized I haven't done much with my life and figured why not move to a completely different part of the country?"

He bursts into laughter at my response. "Okay, well, New York is a large state, and there's a lot of people out here."

I nod my head in agreement.

"Have you made any friends out here?"

"Not really, but my best friend moved out here with me." I look around for Leah, but she is nowhere in sight.

"Tell you what, how about you and I hang out sometime?"

Very straight forward, huh. But making a new friend wouldn't hurt.

"Okay, I'd like that."

"Any plans for the weekend?" he asks, pulling out his phone.

"I'll be hanging out with someone tomorrow night."

"So you have made a new friend then?" he replies, placing both arms behind his back.

"Well, she's not quite a friend yet."

A grin appears at the corners of his mouth.

"Well, how about we discuss future plans for a weekend?"

"That would be great."

"Could I get your number, Cameron?" He extends his phone to me.

I grab my phone and exchange it for his. I input my number into his phone, and he does the same.

"There you go, so I'll expect a text from you today, let's say at 5 o'clock."

I try to suppress a laugh at his unusual specificity, but can't help and let it out. "Why at 5 o'clock?"

"That's what time I get off. We could discuss some ideas I have for our future plans then." I hope these plans doesn't involve anything too draining.

"Talk to you soon, Cameron." He walks away.

"So, I found these jeans, what do you think?"

I turn around and Leah is standing there holding up two pairs, one light blue and one dark blue. I start to point out that she had basically said no to my suggestion of jeans earlier, but stop myself. "I like the darker ones, but the lighter ones might work best."

"Great choice." She hands them over.

As I walk into a fitting room, the realization finally hits me. A beautiful woman asked me out and I did not have to try too hard to impress her. Once I pull the curtain closed, I remove my clothes. I try on the outfit Leah and I selected. It actually looks nice. We didn't do a bad job…and it didn't take four hours.

"Let me see." She starts to pull the curtain open.

"Just a second. I'm coming." I walk out to see Leah looking back at me with her hand on her chin.

"Yeah, I would bring you to meet the parents."

I shake my head at her statement.

"More importantly, I think Riley will like it," I respond.

"Of course, she will!" she shoots back while placing her arm onto my shoulder. "She's going on a date with an amazing guy. What's not to like? Now, let's take a selfie. Smile!" She holds up her cellphone and snaps a photo.

"Okay, let's go eat now; I'm hungry," says Leah

4

HELLO CONFLICT

The food court at the mall has several options, but we narrowed it down to sushi.

"Are you nervous at all about your…whatever you want to call it?" Leah asks between bites.

"Not really; okay, maybe just a bit." I take a sip of tea.

"It'll be great; just try not to overthink it."

Easy for her to say. I remember prom night in high school; I was so worried that my date would not find a dress to match the suit I had. Not only did she not find a dress, but she also canceled on me the week of the event. Talk about heartbreak; not a good feeling to have your date disappear on you without a legitimate excuse other than she is just not that into you.

"You're right, it's going to be a wonderful night." Leah takes a bite of her roll.

"What's up with you and Anthony?"

She rolls her eyes. "We're just peachy, nothing to worry about; we're just one big perfect couple."

By the sarcastic tone, I can tell something is bothering her.

"Okay, what's wrong?" I ask, scooting closer to the table.

"Why would anything be wrong?" She throws the half-eaten sushi roll onto her plate. "Leah."

"Sometimes, I don't even know what we're talking about; the other day he questioned me about my drawer."

Leah and Anthony have been dating for eighteen months. They're both nurses who met right here in this very mall. Leah asked me to go shopping with her one weekend, and while we were browsing, this guy with brown hair, a stocky build, and standing about 5'11" came up to me and asked, "How long have you two been together?" The rest is history.

"Drawer? What exactly was said?" I ask.

"He said to me, 'Why is it I'm allowed to have a drawer only big enough for my underwear?'"

My jaw drops. Her imitation of him sounds about right, however, I don't think that's a reason for her to be upset.

"Like, dude, I said you could have a drawer, not move in. Besides, when he wakes up, he can shower and then just put on his same work clothes after he changes his underwear."

I laugh hysterically.

"Leah, you gave him just an underwear drawer. Do you not see the problem?" She stares at me.

"You're taking your relationship to the next level by allowing him to leave some of his clothes overnight, but instead of letting him bring a change of clothes, he can only bring some socks and underwear?"

She laughs.

"Hey, I never said which drawer he could have, okay? Besides; he hasn't given *me* a drawer."

I roll my eyes.

"It'll work out; just give it time."

She stares at me for a moment.

"Thank you, doctor; anything else you'd like to analyze me on?"

I shake my head. "No, that's it for now." I laugh.

She picks up the other half of her sushi roll and begins chewing. Maybe now is the time to tell her about Reece.

"I met someone in the clothing store."

She chokes on her food and takes a sip of the soda she ordered.

"Again, just look at you. What's her name?" She picks up another piece.

"His name is Reece."

5

HELLO INVITE

Two hours later, I finally make it back to my apartment. Leah and I talk a little more about what she could do for her mom and Anthony. She also asks several questions about Reece that I can't answer. I get a notification alert from my phone. It's a photo of Riley holding up boots and a text that says, "something I picked up to go with my outfit for our night out." She is so adorable. I respond with "excellent choice" and a smiley emoji. I see it that it's 5:01 PM and remember Reece wanted me to text him at 5 PM. I wonder if me texting him now would be too soon. Oh well, here goes nothing. "Hello Reece, Cameron here. It is 5:01, so hopefully you won't be upset about me being a minute late, lol."

As I lie on the couch, I think about what all could go wrong tomorrow night. For example, Riley could bail at the last minute, or I get called into work. Being an EMT can be demanding. Or maybe she'll get called in. Wait, what's her job? I shift my face into the couch. Ugh, why would you agree to hang out with someone and not know what they do or even their last name. My phone rings, and without looking, I answer.

"Hello?"

"Hi, it's Reece."

"Oh, hi Reece."

"How are you, Cameron?"

"I'm doing well. I just got back home. What about yourself?"

"I'm okay, just finishing up with work."

"Awesome. So what's the plan for our weekend?"

"I was thinking a hike and some indoor rock climbing."

What?

"Would this Sunday be okay? We could start at noon."

How about never? Why couldn't he have chosen an amusement park? Even the movies would've been okay. This plan is, well, very active and seems like something that one could easily embarrass themselves at. This is definitely something for me to be nervous about.

"Okay, sounds interesting." I force a laugh.

"Any plans other than a nightclub tomorrow?"

"Not yet. What about you?"

"I'll be working during the day. I'm an optometrist, by the way."

Interesting; I wonder how long he's done that. I think about asking, but maybe I'll save that question for another time.

"Well, I'm excited for Sunday and look forward to an awesome adventure. I'm sure you want to unwind and shower, so we can chat later, if you like?" he suggests in his thick accent that I have yet to place exactly.

"I'm looking forward to it as well. Chat later." I hang up first.

Four hours have gone by since my phone call with Reece. During that time, I watched two foreign films, both with tragic endings. I figure I had better call it a night. As I turn off the TV and head upstairs, I look at my phone and notice a text from Riley and another from Reece. Riley's says, "excited for tomorrow; see you soon." Reece's says, "I am glad I ran into you today, looking forward to an extraordinary adventure." I reply to them both, "me too, goodnight."

HELLO SEXUALITY
Saturday

"What were the other options?" Leah asks, surprised.

"There were no others; he wants to go hiking and indoor rock climbing."

"Don't you think that's a little extreme?" She gets up and walks towards the kitchen, and I follow.

"I should be okay; maybe we'll be around several other people." I pour some tea into a cup.

"Look, you expect me to be okay with you going into the wilderness with a guy you barely know?"

It seems a little odd when she puts it like that, but hey, I am twenty-two. It's something different, and it could be exciting.

"What if you get hurt or mugged?"

She seems so anxious, but I am sure nothing like that will happen.

"I get that you're concerned, but try not to worry so much; I'll be fine."

She shakes her head *no*. "I'm coming with you. No scratch that, Anthony and I are coming with you." She walks back towards the couch.

"Are you serious?" I call after her.

I receive a notification on my phone from Reece. When I open the text, I see a picture of Reece holding a blue rope and smiling. I respond with, "ok, where is mine?" I wait, and a few seconds later, he responds with, "this is yours, mine's orange, lol." I laugh.

Then he actually calls. I was about to make more tea, so I put him on speaker.

"Hello, Reece."

"Hello, are you just as excited as I am for tomorrow?"

"I am. I told my best friend about it, and she's not very excited about the idea."

"Why not?" He laughs.

I sigh and think about what I am going to say. I don't want him to think I have to get her approval, but I also don't want to ignore the possibility of something going wrong. *Stop it, Cameron. Don't overthink it; you will have fun and enjoy this.*

"She doesn't think it's a good idea to be with a stranger alone in nature." The line goes quiet for a bit. Maybe I should not have said that.

"Where is she now?" he asks.

"She's in the living room drinking tea."

"May I speak with her?" he inquires, laughing.

"Just a sec. Leah, can you come here please?"

I hear her set her teacup on the table and then she walks into the kitchen.

"Yes?"

"Someone would like to speak with you." I hand over the phone.

"This is Leah."

She places the phone on the counter and adjusts the volume.

"Hi Leah, I'm Reece, and I was wondering if you'd like to join Cameron and myself tomorrow on our adventure?"

A smirk appears on her face. "Of course. How do you feel about me bringing someone else along?" she says jumping up in excitement.

"The more the merrier."

She looks over to me with her eyes open wide.

"Well, my boyfriend and I shall see you tomorrow." I continue to watch as she tilts her head to the side.

"Can't wait. May I speak with Cameron again?"

She hands me the phone and stares at me with excitement.

"Hey Reece, well, you had the chance to speak with my worried best friend; how was that?"

"It was awesome. Now she can't classify me as a stranger *and* I get to meet the boyfriend. I won't hold you up much longer; I'm still in the store and will look for two more ropes; what color do you think they would like?"

Leah shouts, "Pink for me and brown for Anthony, if they have it." She seems a little too happy about this.

"Did you get that?" I ask Reece.

"I did. I'll look for them. Thanks for the chat, I'll talk to you later." After we end the call, I look up and see Leah still smiling.

"Okay, what is it?" I ask. "You've been excited since the second he spoke." I wait for her to respond.

"That accent…"

"What about it?"

She sighs. "Where did you meet him?" she asks, nudging me with her shoulder.

I grin at her silliness.

"It was at the mall when we were shopping yesterday."

"Wait, that's Reece?" she asks.

Why is she so excited about this guy. Hold on, could it be that she is interested in him? Oh, no. Leah, you have a good guy; please don't mess that up.

"Leah, Anthony is awesome and…"

She looks at me with a frown.

"Cameron, what are you talking about?"

I refuse to let her sabotage her relationship because of her interest in Reece. As her best friend, I feel like it is my responsibility to let her know when she is about to do something irrational or stupid.

"It's not okay for you to dump Anthony so you can go out with Reece," I tell her.

She shakes her head and laughs. I feel like there is a joke I am just not getting.

"What's so funny?" I ask, annoyed.

"I'm sorry, you're misreading me; a guy with a sexy voice on your phone wants to hang out with you alone?"

I wait for her to finish her statement.

"Do you honestly not get what's going on here?"

I shrug; I wish she would say whatever she is thinking.

"He's into you, Cameron."

I open my mouth, shocked by what she has just said. What led her to this conclusion? How can she possibly think a guy I just met yesterday who seems to be exceedingly kind and friendly likes me in that way?

"I think you're mistaken; there was nothing said or done that makes me think he's into me," I respond in his defense.

"Okay." She shrugs her shoulders and hands me back my phone.

She cannot be serious right now; she just accused this man of being into guys, and all she has to say is "Okay."

"No, not okay, Leah. You can't just say stuff like that and expect the conversation to be over with."

She walks away into the living room, and I follow.

"There has to be a reason why you think that."

"You're right. I was totally out of line; I don't know him, so who am I to make that assumption? Can I see a pic of him?" She grabs her cup of tea and sips.

I show her the picture he'd sent to me to save under his contact. She spits out her tea, snatches the phone, and zooms in on the image. She stares at it for a moment, then looks up at me.

"He's hot and he's a ginger. Still think he's into you though." She wipes off some tea drops from my phone and hands it over to me. I ignore her very presumptuous statement and start doing research on my phone about the hiking trail.

7

HELLO CLUB

Three hours have passed and I still have some time to get ready before Riley arrives. Leah left about two hours ago to check on her mom. Looking into Reece's suggestions for sunday, I did not realize there was so much to see on a hiking trail. Hummingbirds, waterfalls, and fields of wildflowers are all within the two-mile hike Reece wants to do. Why don't I ever think of hiking as something for me and Leah to do? I am sure she and I would enjoy it. I'm picturing it now; me ahead of her on a trail and she's asking me to slow down, while trying to catch her breath and catch up. I'm looking for an area with shade. Seconds later, we debate why I chose this place, even though she was just as curious as myself. And Anthony has joined us. He's probably further ahead on the trail than we are. After all, he works out three times a week at the gym. His arms are very toned, and those abs look like they should be on a magazine cover.

Enough of that... Come on, Cameron, time to shower. I head to the bathroom and turn on the radio and listen to a DJ talk about a getaway contest to Maui. I never really understood the fascination people have with these contests. Either way, I will be happy for whoever gets it. As I turn the shower on, I hear my phone ringing. It's probably Leah. I can call her back afterward. I know the water is ready once steam starts covering the mirrors. I check to make sure it's not too hot before getting in. As I step under the spray, the warmth that hits my body feels amazing. I grab my sponge, then squirt some vanilla scent body wash on it. I like using sponges because you get more of a lather, which spreads evenly on your body. I start singing the tune I hear on the radio. Twenty minutes pass before I know it—time to get out.

My phone rings again as I'm getting dressed. With barely one leg in my jeans, I hop over to answer it.

"Cameron?"

"Hey, Reece. Sorry, I was in the shower."

"I just wanted to check in and see if you had any questions for tomorrow's adventures."

"No, everything looks great from what you sent me."

I insert my other leg into my jeans. I put the phone on speaker and set it on top of the toilet tank. I grab the sweater Leah and I chose earlier, pull it on, and scrunch the sleeves up near the elbow. I reach for a comb and knock over the container filled with my toothbrush and toothpaste.

"Is everything okay?" he calls out.

"Yeah, I'm just trying to get ready to head out." I pick up the contents that fell into the sink.

"Ok, well see you tomorrow. Bye."

"Bye."

I attempt to wipe the steamy mirror and smile at my reflection. *It is going to be an awesome hanging out with Riley; you will not overthink or do anything to ruin this night.* These pep talks I give myself work out some of the time.

After spending about five minutes brushing my teeth, I put hair crème on to help my curls become more defined. I glance at the clock and have thirty more minutes to spare—great. That's enough time to call Leah. After three rings, she picks up.

"Leah, I'm freaking out."

"Why?" she yells through the phone.

"What if she comes to her senses and leaves?"

Silence on the other side of the phone.

"Leah?"

"Cam, it'll be fine; there's no need to panic."

"You're right. What are you up to?"

"Well, I was talking with Anthony before you called."

"How'd it go?"

"Absolutely nowhere."

"Just hang in there."

I enjoy the moments like this we have. Usually, we say the same thing to each other whenever either one of us is facing some kind of challenge. My current situation is difficult because I have not been on an actual date in, well, years. After rambling in my head about the different scenarios of what could go wrong, I get a text from Riley saying she is outside. I get very anxious as I walk down the steps to her. When I reach her car, she's sitting there smiling at me. She unlocks the door from the inside, and I get into the passenger seat.

"Are you ready for an amazing night?" she asks.

"I am really happy to be going out and glad it's with someone new."

It takes us about fifteen minutes to get to the nightclub. Before I can pull out the money to pay our entry fee, Riley beats me to it. She turns around, grabs my hand, and we walk inside. The only light seems to be from the fixtures hovering over the bars and the multicolor lights beaming down from the ceiling. She signals for me to follow her to the bar. A guy in a black tank top is busy mixing a drink. He has his back to me. While we wait to get his attention, Riley starts dancing in place.

"I love this song. Do you know it?" she yells while the rather loud music is playing.

"I don't think so, but it's pretty catchy," I say, moving my shoulders from side to side. I am not the best dancer, but I enjoy it, even if I look silly doing it.

"Your moves can use some improvement."

I laugh at her response. "Agreed. I usually just sit on the side and listen to the music when I come here. Sometimes my friend Leah pulls me onto the dance floor and forces me to dance."

The bartender turns around and approaches us. I was not expecting to see him here.

HELLO GOOD TIME

"Cameron, hey! I didn't know you came here," Reece said with a big smile.

It's really nice to see another familiar face, but boy do I have questions about how he ended up behind this bar.

"Yeah, I like the music here and the fact that there's karaoke upstairs," I respond. Riley stands next to me.

"Reece this is Riley."

"Hello there," she says.

"Hello," Reece responds with a chuckle. "What would you both like to drink?"

"Vodka on the rocks," Riley says, turning towards me.

"I'm okay with water for now."

Reece looks at me while tilting his head. "Not a drinker, are you?" he asks.

I shake my head no, and he walks to the opposite end of the bar to get our order. The bar is full of women; I wonder how many have tried to seduce him. He probably gets a lot of attention here—two tip jars-full I bet. But he does not seem to be into the job. I mean, he's not moving to the music at all, nor is he really socializing with any of the guests. And did he lie to me about being an optometrist? I should ask, but then again, we just met; I don't want to be too confrontational. Riley's enjoying herself, though. I can tell by the way she dances. While staring at her, I can't help but think about her beauty and her outfit—a plaid black and white shirt with blue jean shorts and black boots. Since we've been in the club, multiple men *and* women have checked her out.

"Alright, one vodka on the rocks and one water." Reece places both beverages on the counter.

I pull out my credit card, only for him to hold his hand up.

"It's on the house." He winks.

He probably thinks I'm going to get lucky tonight. News flash, buddy—not going to happen. The new way of dating can be a little confusing to me. I felt music and dancing might prevent the awkwardness of me saying something silly. Again, it has been a while.

"Thanks—that's exceedingly kind of you."

"Exceedingly kind of you?" Who says that? If he didn't think I was a goof before, he probably does now. I haven't thought much about our plans for tomorrow. Hopefully Leah won't embarrass herself or me. It would be nice to develop another friend outside of her. I'm not saying I don't have any other relationships. I do like to think that my EMT colleague Jessie, who I usually hang out with on the weekend, is someone who I consider a friend. Leah doesn't feel threatened by our relationship, she considers him as a work friend. She calls our hang outs team-building exercises.

"You're welcome. Let me know if you need anything else." Reece walks away before I can respond.

Riley grabs both of our drinks and hands me mine. We both take a gulp, then she pulls me through the crowd of people. Once we come to a stop, I realize she wanted us on the dance floor. My heart immediately starts racing. Riley begins swinging her hips side to side to the music. She is enjoying herself. To my surprise, she starts grabbing random people and also pulling them onto the dance floor.

"Come on, why are you just standing there?" she asks me over the thumping beat.

Her question catches me by surprise; I didn't think she even noticed me just standing there amidst all the people she was pulling onto the floor. I would say there were at least four others that she managed to get to dance with her. She walks over and grabs my arms until we are both under a light shining in the center. Dancing with her seems to put my thoughts at rest. I am so focused on her beauty; it stops me from worrying about embarrassing her or myself on the dance floor. Maybe no one will notice my awkward dancing.

After thirty minutes of fast-paced music, the DJ switches to something more relaxed. Riley and I stare at each other for a moment. I realize that this could be something great. She opens her mouth to say something to me…

"Could you get me another drink?"

I was hoping for something else. Maybe if I had been a little braver, the moment could have gone differently. I nod my head yes, and leave her on the dance floor. *Excellent job, Cameron. How can you come back from this?* Once I reach the bar, I see that a guy with blonde hair and a black and white t-shirt is now pouring the drinks. He signals he'll be with me in a moment. I turn around, placing my back against the bar, when Reece appears right in front of me.

"Hey Cameron, I was just looking for you."

Why was he looking for me? I notice he has completely changed his outfit. He's now wearing a grey polo shirt with dark-colored slacks. I'm not sure if they are black or navy by the way the lighting keeps changing.

"I'm about to head out. See you tomorrow?"

The club will still be open for another two hours; weird that he's leaving his shift already. It is possible he could be tired or stressed. Based on the bags under his eyes, I will go with tired.

"Okay, sure thing."

He waves, then walks off.

After tapping me, the bartender asks, "What can I get you?" I order another vodka since that is the only drink I know Riley likes; there is still much I don't know about her. After about two minutes, the bartender hands me a glass, then swipes my card. I walk over to the same spot I last saw Riley. She isn't there, so I figure maybe she went to the restroom. I wait fifteen minutes for her to return and then decide it would be better if I walked around to look for her. After twenty minutes, I find her upstairs singing karaoke with some girl. Based on the giggles between each note, slurred singing, and a glass different from what she had before in one hand, it is clear that they are drunk. Before I am able to get closer to the stage, the two kiss. I was not expecting the kiss, let alone one so intimate that it goes on for quite a few seconds. She looks in my direction and waves me over.

"Cameron, this is my girlfriend, Mercedes!"

She is attractive as well. I wonder if Riley surrounds herself with a lot of pretty friends. With her black mid-length hair, Mercedes is giving me a rocker vibe. She and I shake hands. After we are introduced, the two then sing another song together. Once they finish, we decide it is time to go. I end up driving Riley's car due to her being rather intoxicated, and Mercedes has someone else driving her. As I pull up to my apartment complex, I have to yell Riley's name to wake her up.

"I'm fine, you go upstairs," she slurs.

"Riley it's not safe for you to drive like this; just come inside," I plead.

"No, no, no you go inside, I'll be fine handsome." She pinches my cheeks.

"Riley, please…"

After a few moments of silence, she lets out a deep breath.

"Ok, I'll stay the night with you."

Looks like I'll have to help her out of the car and possibly carry her upstairs due to the elevator being out of order. It happens every other week. Once we get inside, I put her in my bed. I figure it would be best to leave her in the same clothes she came through the door in. Then, I get an alert on my cell phone; who could be texting me at two in the morning? To my surprise, it's Reece, wondering if I've made it safely to my destination. I respond with a thumbs up emoji. After a few seconds, he responds with a sleeping emoji followed by "goodnight." I text him several sleeping emojis to indicate my exhaustion, followed by "goodnight" as well.

HELLO DAY AFTER
Sunday

I wake up to a startling, loud thud. Unsure what's going on, I immediately jump up, fists at the ready and prepared for a fight. Looking towards the door, I see Leah standing there.

"Sorry, what's going on here?" she asks, wagging her index finger at my highly defensive and highly unmerited stance.

This could not get any more embarrassing. She is probably hysterically laughing at me on the inside. I'm surprised she's not laughing at me on the outside. Without hesitating, I sit back on the sectional couch, hoping this moment will pass.

"How was last night?" she asks, placing her bag on the coffee table. She then pivots and walks into the kitchen.

I jump off the couch and run behind her. "Sshhh," I whisper.

She spins around looking worried and confused. "What's wrong?" she mouths.

"Riley's here"

"What?!" she shrieks.

I place a finger over my lips. A creek in the floorboards alerts Leah and me. I spin around to Riley creeping towards the front door.

"Good morning," I call out.

She slowly turns around and seems embarrassed.

"Morning," she responds softly.

I look over to Leah, waiting for a response. She nudges her head towards Riley.

"Oh, this is Leah."

They wave to each other and, after a few awkward glances, I walk into the living room and drop down on the couch. I look over to Riley who is staring back at me. As if reading my mind, she comes over and sits next to me.

"I didn't want to wake you…and I figured you would call me once you got up."

Maybe she was trying to be mindful, but part of me wonders if that is true.

Leah walks into the living room and stands near the front door. Could this get any worse? A woman I might really like is sitting here on my couch after having what I would consider a somewhat okay date and probably wondering who the brunette is standing there. Leah, being her natural direct self, walks over to Riley.

"You must be Riley."

Riley extends her hand and shakes Leah's. "Nice to meet you." She looks at me, then back at Leah. "I'm assuming you heard about me since you know my name, but I can't say the same about you." Riley's uncomfortable smile and tone change the mood of the room.

I glance at Leah and notice the sneer appearing on her face. This moment is enough for me to interject, "Leah's my best friend; we've known each other since we were kids." Stepping in between the two, I add, "Sorry I didn't mention that sooner. And we're going on an adventure today, which explains why she's here so early."

Riley nods.

"But I'm not the one who needs introducing." She and Riley continue to stare at each other in silence.

This is not a great first meeting.

Riley finally relents. "Well, I have to go, so I'll call you later. Enjoy the adventure."

"We will," Leah responds.

Riley waves bye and heads out the door.

Leah turns around and stares at me. Whatever she is thinking is not what happened last night. So instead of responding, I head towards the kitchen and she follows. I take out some eggs, spinach, cheddar cheese, and milk, which makes the eggs fluffier. I figured an omelet would be a good choice for breakfast. We have quite a day ahead of us, so it's better to eat something now in case we don't have time for a snack before lunch. Instead of helping me grab two plates and a pan, Leah sits on the bar stool with a smile on her face that I actually can't quite read. Once I finish prepping for the omelet, she starts tapping on the counter.

"Um hello, are you going to tell me what happened, or am I going to have to drag it out of you?!"

As long as I have known Leah, she has not exactly been the most patient person; however, I don't know where to start the story of last night. But I have to say something soon and so I just tell her everything, including running into Reece, as well as the kiss I saw between Riley and her friend.

While cooking the omelet, Leah starts going on and on about what approach I could have taken in each situation. My mind drifts off to Reece. I can't help but wonder what he might think, which is weird. Why am I so concerned about his thoughts?

"Cam!" Leah shouts.

I slide an omelet from the pan onto her plate and give her a fork.

"You had more excitement than me in a week."

I pour two cups of orange juice and sit next to Leah. I take a bite of my omelet.

"Do you think I am attractive?" I ask.

I figure she will be honest with me; we tell each other just about everything. I don't think we have any secrets. I think all types of relationships would last a lifetime if we were honest and open. Whether you're dating, married, or just friends, if you communicate and remain unaffected, any and all of those relationships will survive.

"Of course you are attractive. Why would you even ask that?" She looks at me, waiting for a response.

Instead of replying, I continue to eat my omelet. It is a question I have asked myself many times before. I am not as fit and active as other people. I only go to the gym every other week. I feel my lack of motivation for romance comes from some of these insecurities.

"You are a handsome guy. If we were not friends, I would so have sex with you." We both laugh at her statement.

After sitting in the kitchen talking for almost an hour, I receive a text from Reece about a time change. It looks like he wants to meet up in the next two hours. I respond with "ok" and a thumbs up emoji. While sitting and talking with Leah, a realization hits me.

"Where's Anthony?"

He should have been here by now. Leah did not mention anything about him canceling. She hasn't said much of anything about him since she has been here. I hope these two did not pick today to start a fight. We are making a new friend, and we should probably ease him into our lives without any drama.

"He said he would meet us there."

Based on her tone and an eye-roll, I know something is up. Instead of prying, I inform her about the time change, and she notifies Anthony. Over the next hour, we talk about her mom and how she's doing. Things seem to be improving a little bit. Leah does not seem stressed. In the middle of our conversation, we end up changing into our hiking clothes; she in the restroom while I do so in the bedroom. We decide to ride together to have more time to chat about whatever was bothering her about Anthony. The conclusion is he just seems distant, and she feels like maybe he is getting tired of her. I assure her that cannot be the case. The way he looks at her, I am surprised he has not popped the question yet.

10

HELLO ADVENTURE

After arriving at the indoor rock-climbing center, I text Reece to let him know we're here.

He responds with, "I am waiting inside, right by the door." As Leah and I get out of the car, I notice Anthony walking towards us. Looking at his facial expression, you can tell that he is bothered by his drama with Leah.

"Hey, Anthony. I'm gonna go find Reece."

Under other conditions, I would have happily been their third wheel, but figure it is best to give those two some space. As soon as I walk through the door, Reece stands up and immediately embraces me. I see now I am dealing with someone who likes hugs. He smells nice, and I wonder what his scent is. He has on a white and grey tank top with grey shorts and white tennis shoes. His arms look good. I wonder how often he works out; I may have to ask for his meal and workout plan.

"Where's Leah and her boyfriend?" he asks with concern.

He seems so sincere and kind. It might take me some getting use to the accent. For some time now, I've wondered what it is exactly; not that it's essential to know, but I am curious.

"They're outside… So where are you from?" Maybe this will buy more time before he gets suspicious about them. There goes that grin of his again. I cannot quite explain why, but it is pretty calming.

"I'm from Ireland; Galway, to be exact."

"What brought you to the US? That's a pretty big jump."

He simply says, "Life changes," and stares at me for a moment.

"Um, how long have you been here?"

"A year now."

I nod my head at his response and then look towards the door; Still no Leah and Anthony.

Quick Cameron, think of something.

"So how did you find this place?"

I wish Leah and Anthony would hurry up. Why today of all days did they have to hash out their problems?

"I discovered this place on my way from work about three months ago."

"Do you usually come alone?"

I look to my right and notice someone sitting on the bench bandaging a wound. Reece follows my view.

"I do…and don't worry; I won't let you get hurt," he says with a small grin appearing on his face.

Anthony and Leah finally walk in. I wave my hand to get their attention. Leah struts right up to Reece.

"Hello, I'm Leah, nice to meet you." She wraps her arms around him.

Anthony's jaw clenches. "I'm her boyfriend, Anthony." He and Reece shake hands.

"I'm Reece. Nice to meet you both in person."

I can see the irritation on Leah's face. What happened out there?

"Alright, everyone, follow me!" Reece shouts. He then provides us all with the ropes he purchased and a tour telling us the rules while inside the building. It lasts for thirty minutes. Even after all of that, I still don't feel very prepared, but at least we have an experienced climber to ensure our safety.

Seemingly anxious to get started, Reece asks, "Who wants to go first?"

The three of us just look at each other. I've never done this before and neither have Leah or Anthony; I think it is safe to say that none of us wants to go first. I look around at the other people scaling the walls and see how comfortable they are; even the teenagers. I notice a section upstairs with hardly anyone up there and fewer rocks to climb.

"I'll go, but how about we try it up there," I suggest, pointing at the sparsely populated area.

Reece looks in that direction and laughs. I thought it was a good spot, so I'm confused about why he thinks this is funny. Based on Leah's expression, I would guess she is just as bewildered by his reaction. She raises her eyebrow and mouths, "Awkward." I grin and mouth, "Stop."

"That's for children." He continues to laugh.

Children go rock-climbing? What happened to hide and seek, freeze tag, 1-2-3 Not It? I know things are a little different from my childhood now, but come on.

"How about over there?" He gestures towards an empty corner.

It is a high climb to attempt, but it's a slightly more private area. There's less of an audience to be embarrassed in front of. And at least people will be safe from us if we fall.

"Let's go." I lead the way, hoping that before we get over there, Leah or Anthony will object. Of course, neither of them says anything, so we all continue to walk over.

Once we reach the spot, my heart starts pounding. Okay, it might have been a bad idea; I mean, come on, I am not a professional athlete, and the tutorial he provided could have been more detailed.

"Since we're inexperienced, maybe you should go first, Reece." I spin around and wait for him to respond. He seems so calm and focused; it is apparent he feels pretty confident about this sport. Anthony and Leah nod their head in agreement. It would have been better if they had spoken up, too.

"Someone has to ensure the rope is secured, and since none of you have done this before, I think it'll be better if you climb now, and that way I can let you down safely."

While that seems to be a valid point, it still does not put my mind at ease. But I did say I wanted to start a new life… I just did not expect this new life to have significant risks so soon. Come on, Cameron, you got this. As I stand there, Reece begins adjusting my rope and harness. The others just stand there watching. I notice a wink from Leah. Her assumptions of Reece liking me still linger in my head. I am not one to judge, but I wonder if I should ask him to clarify things now or later.

"Okay, Cameron, listen up; each rock is color-coordinated, so make sure you stick with one color; otherwise, it will make your climb a lot more difficult."

Okay, stick with a single color, Cameron. Easy. You can do that. I notice some rocks are trickier than others. After looking at the color chart, the blue ones seem to be for beginners; so blue it is. I pull myself up with the first rock. Halfway through the motion, I notice that the next blue rock is pretty far away. He said to stick with one color, but that purple one is much closer. Not realizing how long I've been completely stationary, I hear Reece's voice and it startles me.

"Are you okay?"

I am really nervous and really focused at the same time. I don't want to chicken out, so I go for it. But after reaching for the other rock, I lose my balance on the one beneath my feet, and while trying to regain my balance, I start to panic.

"Breathe, Cameron. You got this!" Reece yells.

Easy for him to say; he's not the one up here scared. After failing to regain my balance on the blue rock, I decide to go for the purple. My strategy might be a big mistake though, my right hand is on a purple rock and my left foot is on a green one. I must get my breathing under control; I don't want to pass out up here. *One, two, three, four, five, six, seven. Eight… Nine…*

"Cameron, don't move; I'm coming up."

I look down and see Reece talking to Anthony. I quickly turn my head back towards the stones. I didn't realize how far I had made it. *Please don't fall, please don't fall.* I attempt to pull myself up but to no avail. My arms are tired. My breathing rate picks up. I look towards the others and notice Reece and Anthony switching ropes and harnesses. What is he doing? I can do this without help. I try to climb up on the next closest rock I see, but that only makes things more difficult.

"Cameron, stay still," Leah shouts with concern. "Reece is coming."

Simply outstanding. On my first attempt at rock-climbing, I need saving. I lean my forehead against the rock in front of me and begin to count.

"One, two, three, four, five, six, seven, eight"

"How are you holding up?" Reece grabs onto my shoulder.

I just want to get down quickly. "Well, it could be better, but I'm okay." Seeing him brings a sigh of relief, but I feel lightheaded.

"Let's get you down from here." He moves closer to me.

"Ok, you're going to place your feet like this."

I watch as he adjusts his feet on the wall.

"Then you're going to release some of your rope little by little." I continue to watch as he releases some rope from the latch.

"Then kick from the wall."

I nod my head in agreement.

"Anthony, now," he says.

He instructs me as I continue to shift myself backwards and adjust my rope. I am not okay with this. However, he has been doing this for way longer than I have, so I guess this is where the trust comes in.

"I'm not going to let you get hurt."

I continue releasing some rope. This is new to me and not what I expected. I'm putting my trust in a guy I barely even know with my safety…my life maybe.

"Now, use your legs to push yourself off the wall, but we're going to take small jumps on the way down."

Okay, I can do those small jumps; they don't sound too painful or difficult. I kick myself off the wall but panic when I drop a few inches.

"I can't do this!" I scream.

Reece follows and grabs my hand. "Look at me—I'm right here." he says softly.

Gazing into his eyes provides me with comfort. He continues to hold my hand.

"Let's go."

We drop in unison. It takes us about five minutes to make it to the ground. Leah immediately jumps and hugs me.

She turns to Reece and announces, "I don't like this; we should leave now."

As much as I agree, we just got here, and I don't want to be the one to ruin anybody's fun.

"We agreed on new beginnings," I announce. "And I think we should stay." With that, she rolls her eyes and walks back over to Anthony.

"Oh, come on, Leah. I made it halfway and surprised myself. Don't you want to see what you're capable of, beautiful?"

A slight grin appears on her face. "Well, since you put it that way, I guess it wouldn't hurt for 'beautiful' to put on a show," she acknowledges laughing.

Next up was Leah, then Anthony. Leah makes it further than I did, and Anthony of course, climbed it all the way to the top. Reece was supposed to be the last to go but decides not to since we're still unfamiliar with handling the rope.

In spite of it all, I'm enjoying myself. I conquered my fear of heights. Okay, maybe not completely.

We walk around for a while to see the different obstacles the complex has. The free-climbing wall is a little alarming; I wonder what safety precautions they have for people who actually fall. Reece assures me that anyone climbing is certified. After touring the place, we decide it's time to start the next activity. I'm excited about the hiking, but also nervous because I hope Leah and Anthony will remain on their best behavior. Not sure if this activity is a great idea for these two right now.

HELLO NATURE

I end up driving to the trail alone. Anthony wanted Leah to ride with him. She hesitantly agreed. My cell starts to ring, and without looking, I pick it up.

"Hello?"

"Hi, Cameron," Riley calls out through the phone.

"How are you?"

"I'm okay, and yourself? Have you started your adventure yet?"

"I'm alright...I'm heading up to a trail with some friends as we speak."

"Okay, I wanted to let you know I really enjoyed myself last night; I'm excited to spend more time with you."

I was still unsure what to make of her exit this morning. I didn't think I would hear back from her today, but this seems to confirm there will be a next time.

"I also want to apologize for how drunk I got, I'm not usually like that...it's just been so long since I've enjoyed myself."

She goes on and on about her and Mercedes and what they have planned today. Should I be jealous that she sounds more excited to spend time with her friend? I mean, we are in the beginning stage of this.

"So, when did you want to get together again?" I ask.

"Anytime next week works for me."

"Okay, well, we can discuss an exact day later today; I'm pulling up to the trail; talk to you soon."

"Okay Cameron—later."

This gal is fantastic; I'm so excited I met her. It's been a long time since I've felt this way. The thought of it all gives me a lovely, bubbly feeling inside. Could she be the one? *No wait—let's not jump ahead Cameron. Just enjoy the now.*

From the parking lot I see trees, a lake, a bridge, birds flying, and hear laughter. I pull into the first spot I see available in the parking lot. I notice Anthony and Leah parked four spots over, getting out of their car. As I make my way over to them, I overhear the two arguing. I decide to get a little closer. Is it wrong for me to spy on my best friend and her boyfriend? I cannot shake the feeling that she is not telling me everything.

"You need to grow up. Nothing is going on," Leah yells. "Why can't you just believe me?"

Anthony slams the door. I don't think there has been a time that I have ever witnessed him so upset. He is usually calm and polite, and always very charming towards Leah. He's the kind of guy who opens doors for her, pulls out her chair, is fast with a compliment. You know, the kind of stuff you expect from Prince Charming.

"I would believe you if you weren't being so secretive," Anthony says slamming the door. "But how can I when you're giving me every reason not to?"

Leah responds by slamming her door as well. I have got to intervene before this gets any worse. Without a second thought, I run over to them.

"Hey, guys! Ready for the hike?" I chirp.

I did not think entirely through about what to say, but acting fast was the priority. It was either that or stand there and watch my best friend's relationship fall apart in front of my eyes.

"Anthony and I have decided to let you and Reece enjoy this alone. We're leaving." Leah hugs me, then gets back into the car.

I stare at her and Anthony in disbelief. No, this cannot happen; I refuse to let this happen.

"So sorry Cameron, we're just having a difficult time right now. We'll talk later, yeah?"

As if I have a choice; both of their minds seem made up. Anthony gets behind the steering wheel, immediately starts the engine, and pulls off.

"Are they going to be okay?" I turn around and notice Reece standing there with a concerned look.

"Oh yeah, they just need to talk about some things," I reply sheepishly. "Are you ready?"

"I am, but are you?"

"Yeah, yeah."

I am not. What if I pass out from dehydration? And what about the many wild animals that call this area home? Wait a minute—what if there's a poisonous sna—

"C'mon, Cameron…let's go."

"Okay."

HELLO QUESTIONS

Well, Reece actually wasn't so ready. He forgot his backpack for the trail, so I wait on the bench for him. In the meantime, Riley manages to keep me company. She texted me a photo of her and Mercedes blowing kisses from some restaurant they went to. I respond with a heart emoji. I hope she likes it.

"Got it," Reece announces and then sits next to me.

I am sure he does not have any problems getting a girl…or guy. I wonder if it'd be appropriate to ask him about his personal life? It is just the two of us now. I don't see why he would be offended. Then again, it might come off rude asking another man if he likes men.

"So, is everything good now?"

I'm assuming he's referring to Leah and Anthony. Part of me wants to say yes, but the other wants to say that I don't know and that I should go after her. But Reece planned an incredible day for us to hang out, and I don't want to seem rude or unappreciative.

"Can we talk about something else?" I feel like that's the appropriate route to take in changing the subject. "So, are you single?" I was anxious to know; curiosity was getting the best of me and I thought I'd broach the subject diplomatically.

He smiles at my question. Whoa, he has dimples for days. How did I not notice them before? *No, don't get distracted Cameron. Focus on the question and wait for a response.*

"I am. Are you?"

Dammit, I guess that was a failure; now what? Do I answer the question or respond with a follow-up?

"Yes, going on two years now," I reply. "How long has it been for you?"

"It's been three years. I find it a little difficult to date." He pulls out two water bottles and hands me one. We both take a sip. "Some people just don't like to take the time and get to know someone," he adds. "And they're so quick to get in bed with you."

I cannot relate. I don't find myself in the dating scene much.

"I want someone passionate, adventurous, spontaneous, observant…" he continues. "I can go on and on, but it won't change anything." He takes another sip of his water. He looks sad.

"You'll find her; it just takes time." I begin drinking more water.

I cannot believe I even thought for a moment he— "…or him," he responds, grinning.

I choke on some water. He begins patting my back. I wipe my lips with the back of my hand.

I look over to him and find his piercing grey eyes staring back at me.

"I drank it too fast." I laugh nervously.

He removes his hand and stands up. "Let's go."

Forty-five minutes pass and we're halfway through the hike, at least I think we are. The scenery is lovely. There is a beautiful stream nearby and I pull out my phone to take a picture.

"Gorgeous, right?" Reece says, gazing at the view.

"It is." I smile as some birds fly by.

"Come on."

I follow as he leads the way. The trail begins to incline rather steeply, so I grab the nearest branch. It snaps. I slip, scraping my hand on a rock as I slide down towards the level ground.

"Argh!" I look at my hand to see a gash.

Reece turns around and runs towards me. "Let me take a look." He presses on the wound a little. I yell out in pain. He removes his bag and pulls out a first-aid kit. After retrieving a mini brown bottle from the kit, he squeezes some liquid from it on my hand.

"Aghhh! What is that?"

"Peroxide, hold still." He then begins pat drying the excess fluid. "It doesn't look like there's anything inside the wound." He begins wrapping my hand with some bandages.

"Do you mind if we stop here for a moment?" I ask.

"Sure." He sits next to me.

I pull the water bottle out of the backpack, and down a few gulps. One thing I can say about this hike is it takes a lot out of you. My clothes are completely soaked.

'How are you holding up?" Reece asks while grabbing my bottle and chugging from it.

First, he admitted that he has an interest in guys, which is no problem, but now he's drinking from the same bottle as me. I cannot shake the feeling that he thinks this is more than just two guys hanging out. I like Reece. I think he is a fun guy, and we could have more adventures like this, but I don't want to give him the wrong impression. I also don't want to say anything that may affect our friendship, so I decide to play it safe.

"I'm great Reece, what about you?"

He stands up, and starts running further along the trail.

I thought we were resting for a moment.

"Hey, wait up." I quickly get up and follow. I grab onto another branch that looks sturdier and pull myself up the incline trail.

He is fast, and I was not expecting to run during this hike. At this rate, I'll tire myself, so I slow down my pace.

"Reece!" I call out.

I bend over to catch my breath. After a few seconds I look up and he is still nowhere in sight. All I see is a lot of trees. In addition to cracking branches, I hear frogs, insects, and what also could be a snake. Wait, what if that was a bear? I hear another branch crack. It's getting closer. My breathing begins to quicken and my chest tightens.

"Reece…" I murmur.

I collapse on the ground. I hear footsteps and look up to see a silhouette standing above me blocking out the sun.

"Cameron, what's wrong?"

Reece kneels and lifts me into his lap.

"I couldn't keep up and…"

I black out after that.

Waking up, I somehow find myself on Reece's back while he continues to hike. I have no idea how long I've been in this position.

"Um, Reece, you don't have to…"

"It's my fault. I shouldn't have made you…I'm sorry."

I get myself off Reece. His face is very red, so I pull a bottle of water out and hand it to him. He takes a large gulp.

"Sorry if I was too heavy," I murmur.

He smirks and hands me back the bottle. "Let's keep going."

We walk for another thirty minutes and, at this point, Reece is a few feet ahead of me.

"We made it!" he shouts.

I turn my attention to where he's looking. A sigh of relief hits me as I read the sign: "Your Journey Ends Here." Well, it was a nice hiking trail, but it is time for us to go.

"You did it, Cameron; very impressive."

Judging by his tone, I would say he doubted that I was going to make it to the end of the trail.

"You didn't think I would finish?" I question. A little insulting. I mean, yeah, I could not finish the rock climb, and I may have fallen behind on the hike, and maybe I spent a portion of it blacked out on his back, but he could at least give me some credit for being determined.

"Well, sorry to break it to you, Reece, but it looks like you have a competitive challenger on your turf now." My legs are burning, I take a seat on the ground hoping to catch my breath. Man, I'm out of shape. He laughs while watching me. That's something else about him; his smile and how good-natured he seems. "So, what now?" I ask.

He stares at me for a moment and then responds, "Let's eat; I packed lunch."

I follow Reece as he walks over to a thicker patch of grass and sets down his bag. From it, he pulls out a red and white picnic blanket, and lays it on the ground, taking care to avoid crushing some daisies. The view here is spectacular. We found a spot on top of a hill near the center of the park. Birds are flying above us while the sun sets. Reece has made tuna sandwiches and packed chips, tea, and juice, as well as a board game and a pack of cards. We sit on the blanket, laughing and talking about what things were like growing up as kids. We bond over Cheetos. It turns out we both favor them over other chips. He's into country music like me. We also discuss his work as an optometrist and mine as an EMT. And he lets me know that he helps out at the bar of the nightclub since a buddy of his owns it. So that's one mystery down.

"If you could choose one word to describe yourself, what would it be?" I ask.

He thinks for a moment before responding.

"Accepting, that's what I would I say. What would you choose?"

Usually, I am the one asking questions and getting answers. If I had to pick one word, what would it be? Maybe driven, passionate, empathetic, oh wait, I know…

"Considerate"

He nods his head as if he agrees. Time is passing so quickly; a couple of hours have gone by, and here we are still asking questions about each other. But now, the outside world is starting to creep in and I wonder if Leah and Anthony are okay.

As if reading my mind, he asks, "Do you think your friends have had time to cool off?"

It has been a few hours since we last spoke and it's not like Leah to not check in with me in that kind of time frame. Although things seemed intense, by now she would have made a joke or texted something silly. Silence is something she does not do for long.

"I don't know. And sorry about the scene earlier."

He waves his hand. "No need to apologize. I'm glad you stayed; I enjoyed getting to know you more."

I enjoyed getting to know him better as well, and we have so much in common.

"Same here; I think it's interesting how fascinated you are by *The Sims*," I respond with a laugh. He seems borderline obsessed by the game and talked about it for quite a while after the Cheetos conversation.

"Look, you can't say it isn't mind-blowing to have a life set exactly how you want it to be," he manages to say in between laughs.

I guess I can't say I disagree.

"Thank you Reece. This was nice. Glad I was able to make another amazing friend." He nods and takes another sip of his beverage.

"Well, guess our time here is up," I offer.

He turns toward me and says, "No, it's just beginning."

Reece and I start to pack once we feel some rain droplets. Today was a great day. I rock-climbed, hiked, and had a picnic. I had the opportunity to get to know a fantastic guy. Although we have similarities, we are entirely different. For example, he's very into nature, and I'm not. He's adventurous, and I'm cautious. One thing we both agree on is settling down and starting a family.

While putting his belongings in his car, I notice a tattoo behind his ear. It reads, "Listen." I don't want to overload him with questions, so I'll save that for another day.

"Thank you for hanging out with me Cameron. You're a great guy. So, any plans for next week?" Riley and I are supposed to do something, but we don't have an exact day.

"Nothing set officially; do you have anything in mind?" I ask.

Whatever you do, please don't mention rock climbing.

He raises an eyebrow and says with a smirk, "Laser Tag."

Laser Tag? Why would he suggest that? I've seen commercials, and those places look rather dark and scary.

"Yeah, that sounds cool."

Cool! Did that just come out of my mouth? What is wrong with you Cameron? It's a wonder he doesn't think I'm lame yet. I'm sure he's laughing at me on the inside. "Okay, we'll discuss more details later then? Get home safe." We wave and get into our cars.

HELLO BREAK-UP

I pull into the parking garage and recognize Leah's car. Walking towards the elevator, I realize she's still inside her car and just sitting there crying. I don't like seeing my friend like this. Between the two of us, she's usually the fun one. I think it's time for some answers. I walk over and tap on the window. She's startled, but then gets out of the car. Before I can say anything, she immediately hugs me.

"Leah, what's going on?"

She lets go of me, then turns away. The silence is driving me a little insane. Come on Leah, just say it. Are you two breaking up? I hope not. I like Anthony for her. He's much nicer than some guys she's dated in the past.

"I'm pregnant."

I take a step back, shocked at what I've just heard.

"Since when?"

Why is this something I'm just finding out now?

"I took a test last night. Before that, I'd suspected I might be, but I didn't know how to tell you."

"Let's talk inside."

I grab her hand and we walk up several flights of stairs until we reach my door. I open it and follow Leah as she goes inside. She sits on the sofa.

"I've been feeling sick lately," she explains, grabbing her stomach. "I thought maybe it was due to the stress of checking in on Mom and work."

How did I not notice this?

"Then I began throwing up every morning and started to suspect…"

I stand against the wall, unsure of what to say or where to start.

"I started feeling like this a week ago."

I take a seat next to her and hold both her hands.

"Also…I haven't mentioned any of this to Anthony."

"What, why not?" I can't contain my frustration. "Eighteen months Leah… You've been together a year and a half. He deserves to know."

She jumps up and heads towards the kitchen, and I follow her. It's like she doesn't want him to know, almost as if she has no intention of telling him.

"Are you listening to me?"

She grabs a soda out of the fridge, then slams the door.

"Yes!" she screams. "What do you expect me to say, Cam? 'Anthony I'm pregnant, and by the way, I'm not sure if I want to start a family with you.'"

There it is; she's not upset about being pregnant; she doesn't think she and Anthony can make it.

"Look, you both love each other," I offer, trying my best to calm and assure her.

"That's the issue, Cam; I don't know if I still love him."

I wasn't expecting that. Yeah, they have their problems like any other couple, but I didn't think she would fall out of love with Anthony. She sits on the bar stool, looking down and holding her head with both hands. I walk over and take a stool next to her and we sit in silence. She gets a text message and, judging by her face, it's probably Anthony. She goes into the bathroom and shuts the door. I receive two notifications. The first one is Riley saying, "let's hang Friday" and the other is from Reece, "what about Friday?" The timing between these two… I respond to both with "what time?"

Fifteen minutes pass by before Leah comes out in tears. I walk over to her and begin to cry as well. It kills me to see her like this. She goes into the kitchen and leans on the bar.

"It's over… Anthony and I are over."

I pull her into a hug.

"I'm not crying because of the breakup; I'm sad because my baby may grow up without a father."

I don't think she's right; Anthony doesn't seem like that kind of guy. I brush her hair back behind her ears.

"It's okay, you have me, so a father figure will still be there." After all, I would never abandon her.

"Good, that'll make it easier." She squeezes me tighter.

"So, did he say he didn't want a child?"

She releases me and turns away.

"No, he didn't." She starts biting her fingernails.

She's not telling me the whole story; there has to be more to the conversation. She starts pacing back and forth. Come on, Leah, just tell me already, what could have you so worked up? I block her path and stand there firmly, waiting for a response.

"I…I wanted to tell him, I really did but…"

What? I couldn't believe it, something like this should not be kept secret. The only logical thing to do is to take action. Before she can say anything else, I immediately pull out my phone and start to call Anthony, but she quickly grabs it out of my hands.

"Leah, this is serious. How can you be okay with this?"

She stands there saying nothing, but then goes over to the couch and sits down. I wait for a response, but nothing. An alert on my phone breaks through the silence.

"Give me back my phone please."

She sticks it behind the cushion.

"Not until I know for certain you won't mention the pregnancy to Anthony."

Why would she do this? He deserves to know. She is making a huge mistake, but who am I to tell her what to do? The only thing I can do is stand by. I'm in no place to judge. Although I can't entirely agree with this decision, I have to respect it.

"Okay, you're right; it's not my place to say anything to him about his child, so I'll let you deal with it."

She hands me my phone and crosses her legs. I hope part of her knows that I'm right about this. The message I received was from Reece saying "let's do 7:00 PM." I respond with "ok, text me the address" and place my cell in my pocket, then look back at Leah. The sadness in her eyes tells me not only does she know it's a mistake not to say anything to him, but also that she's afraid. I sit down on the couch and put my arm around her. Leah turns to hug me and we just sit there holding each other.

HELLO DAMAGE CONTROL
Monday

It's the next day and Leah and I are still on the couch. She cried herself to sleep. I didn't want to leave her alone, so instead of going to work, I called in sick and stayed with her.

I decide to make breakfast. Leah is still asleep, so I write her a note and head out to pick up some orange juice. The ten-minute drive to the grocery store is relaxing. I use that time to think, and what I'm thinking right now is, how can I help my friend? I know I told her I wouldn't say anything to Anthony, but I *didn't* say I wouldn't help. I can't just stand by and leave someone I love to suffer.

As I pull into the parking lot, I encounter a lot of cars and barely any spots to park. It's so crowded today. Walking into the store, I see the check-out lines snaking around. Oh well, I still want orange juice. I'm barely inside when I feel a tap on my shoulder, it's Riley standing there, smiling in blue jean cut-off shorts and a pink blouse.

"Hey Cameron, I see great minds think alike." She laughs.

She has a beautiful smile; I wonder how long she's been single or, more importantly, *if* she's single. And while I would consider our hang-out the other night a date, I wonder if she does. I know—I'm overthinking it. I should just let it casually flow. I'm working on it. I haven't been out in the dating field for quite some time.

"What are you getting? Mercedes and I plan on making nachos tonight."

"I came to get orange juice; I'm making Leah breakfast."

I mean, Riley could invite me over for nachos, but I get it she wants to hang out with her friend. I wonder how long they've known each other.

"So, nachos, huh? What do you need for that?" I ask while stepping aside for an older woman to get through. We probably should move from the entrance.

"Just the chips; we have everything else we need in the pantry, but I'm going to get some other things for the rest of the week." Signaling me to follow her, she adds, "Let's move; it's getting a little crowded."

"I like getting your texts, but it's nice to get to see you in person." We shift a little more to the right to let a woman and a child pass by.

"I know I wrote you, but I feel like I should say this in person," she says.

Say what?

"I'm sorry about my behavior the other night," she says, starting to walk down the aisle.

"It's been some time since I went out and enjoyed myself like that. I hope you won't let that affect your opinion of me."

I wave my hands in front of me.

"Not at all, I'm glad you had fun."

Once we make it to the end of the aisle, I see the juice and grab it.

"Would you be interested in having frozen yogurt with me?" she asks cautiously.

A second date, so awesome. At that moment, I trip over my feet and faceplant into the floor.

"Cam!"

Riley quickly kneels in front of me and I turn my head up. I stare into her hazel eyes before looking to her lips. Oh, how badly I wish they were pressed against mine. I roll onto my side and she grabs both my arms to pull me up a bit and I use my legs to propel myself the rest of the way.

"Are you hurt?" she asks, analyzing my nose then elbows and knees.

"I don't see any wounds."

"I'm okay," I assure her.

She places her hands on both of my cheeks.

"So, Friday at 3:00 PM?" she asks.

"I'd like that."

We continue walking throughout the store, grabbing the groceries she needed. But the whole time, the conversation is flowing. I find out that she crashed her dad's car into the mailbox when she was seventeen, that she has an older brother named Miguel, and that she's a mechanic. A mechanic? How cool is that?

"Well Cam, I'm looking forward to our next hangout." She tucks her hair behind her ear while looking down.

"I am, too." I can't help but look down as well.

"I hope the nachos turn out great."

She chuckles.

"Let me know when you make it home." She gives my arm a little squeeze and walks away.

Hopefully, by the time I make it back to the apartment, Leah will be up. After all, it is 10 AM. I end up buying some sauce and pasta for the alfredo dish I've decided to make tonight. I already have garlic bread in the freezer.

Once home, I see Leah at the kitchen table, eating the breakfast I had prepared.

"Couldn't wait for the orange juice?"

She looks up and rolls her eyes. Maybe she's feeling a little better. Last night was a lot to take in. I don't want to ruin the moment by bringing it up, so instead I pour a glass of juice and start eating with her.

"Aren't you going to heat that up?" Leah points at my plate.

I don't mind cold breakfast; it still tastes fresh to me, it's just not as hot.

"What for, it tastes amazing?" I put a fork full of eggs in my mouth.

"So, what's on the agenda today?"

She plays with her food a bit, then shrugs her shoulders.

"Maybe we can go for a walk or go shopping."

Her face lights up with joy at the word "shopping." That probably should've been my first suggestion. Leah enjoys shopping for others as much as herself. My wardrobe is full of clothes that she thought would look great on me.

"Cameron, darling, of course. Let's get dressed."

I'm so glad to see some of her old spirit return. She runs towards my bedroom to see what she can find to wear. Leah and I have been best friends since we were kids, so she does have her own drawer here with some of her clothes. Also, part of the closet is hers. And there's space for some of my things at her apartment as well. When we first moved to Rochester, we got this place together, but she decided to move out so she and Anthony could have more time and space to themselves. Twenty minutes later, she comes out wearing khaki shorts, a white blouse, and brown sandals.

"Why haven't you changed?"

Instead of responding, I just sit there and laugh.

"Cam!" she shouts.

"There's nothing wrong with what I'm wearing." I have on a pair of shorts and a t-shirt with some decent sneakers on my feet.

"We're shopping—who knows who we might run into. And maybe we'll stop and eat somewhere nice."

"Leah…"

"No—go change clothes now!"

The clothing store we decided to go to is packed. So many other guys here just have on t-shirts and shorts. I should've ignored Leah. Instead, I changed and put on a polo and some khaki shorts. I manage to find a pair of olive-green slacks that I want to try on. Leah is still looking at shoes, so I decide to browse around some more. The selection of clothes in this place could take hours to look through. There's a second floor with more options and I decide to take the stairs instead of the elevator. The shoes for men here usually seem over-priced, but right now there's a buy-one-get-one sale for

$40. Buying two pairs of shoes here would be about the same price I would typically spend on one pair.

"Cameron—hey." I turn around to see Reece.

Without hesitation, we immediately fall into a hug. I feel comfortable with him. Judging by the number of items he's holding, he's been in here for a while.

"Hey, how are you?" I ask.

He swings the clothes over his shoulder and smirks as if I made a joke. He walks over to some jeans and signals me to follow.

"I'm doing well, just shopping for some work clothes; being an upstanding optometrist in the community can get pricey," he says, laughing. "You've got to dress to impress. And let's not forget the dry-cleaning bills."

Each time we've gotten together, he seems to bring out a different side of me; it's nice to feel and do something different.

"I'm doing the same, well, except as an EMT, we have uniforms already."

He didn't seem to find that funny, but then I guess it wasn't. *Come on Cameron; swim before you sink. Think of something else to say before the conversation dies out.*

"Leah and I are just having some bonding time. Not much to do today, so we figured we would do some shopping. She's downstairs."

"That's awesome."

He picks up a pair of jeans.

"What do you think about these?"

Well, they're rust-colored, but I think he can pull it off. I, on the other, am only good with light blue jeans.

"I like them for you; maybe wear them with a button-up shirt."

He nods his head and places the pair of jeans on his shoulder and continues browsing.

"I'll get a basket; you look like you could use one."

His smile confirms I was right, so I walk towards the elevator and find one lone basket left.

It was meant to be. Once I return, he immediately places all the clothes inside.

"Thanks lad. So are you ready for Laser Tag this Friday?"

I haven't put much thought into it. I do like the idea of doing something different and out of my comfort zone. Who knows? Maybe this will bring out a competitive side of me I didn't know existed.

"I am, but the question is, are you?"

He stares at me for a moment.

"Of course, but I'll make sure not to hurt you."

What makes him think he can hurt me? Well, he probably could.

"I guess I'll have to put that ego of yours in its place."

My response has no impact on him. Instead, he just continues to stare. I'll admit, I am starting to get a little intimidated.

"I guess we'll see who's more dominant." With that, he pulls back and continues searching through the jeans.

"Cameron," I hear Leah yell, and turn to see her coming from the elevator.

"Did you find anything?"

Judging by the lack of clothing in her hand, she couldn't find anything she wanted. Usually, Leah will have an entire outfit put together before I can find anything interesting.

"No, I didn't, but look who I ran into."

As soon as she sees Reece, excitement lights up her face. And without any hesitation, she walks right over and hugs him.

"Reece, hey. Nice to see you. Look, I want to apologize for backing out on our plans the other day."

He shakes his head.

"It's okay. Cameron and I still had a good time. I'm sure we'll see more of each other."

She then glares at me.

"Agreed. So what are we looking for?"

It was only a matter of time before take-charge Leah surfaced, but I had figured it would be of me, not Reece.

"Just looking for more work clothes."

If only he knew the shopping marathon he was just about to provoke.

"Well, sweetie, I can help you with that."

15

HELLO BONDING

"I think anything pastel is your color."

Leah has been saying this to me for years. The results are usually the same. She gets a basket filled with a variety of pastel-colored clothes and expects me to try them all on. So here I am in the fitting room, waiting for a space to become available with Reece.

"I'm going to look at some more stuff. I'll be right back."

She walks away, leaving Reece and me standing here.

"So, Reece, we haven't talked much about your work; how long have you been an optometrist?"

I know it's a straightforward question, but if you want answers, you have to start somewhere. He seems very open and honest.

"Two years. My dad was an optometrist; I enjoyed visiting his work and helping people see the beauty life has to offer, which is also the reason why I'm really into in all kinds of nature activities."

I can attest to that.

"What about you Cameron? How long have you been an EMT?"

The line for a dressing room starts moving, and I notice that Reece is up next.

"Three years. I knew I wanted to be a part of the medical field since I was a teenager; I've never really been a fan of being helpless, so I figure if I can learn something that can help in any medical situation, why not?"

"Next. How many?" the fitting room associate asks Reece.

"Well, between mine and his, I'd say way over thirty items," he announces, laughing.

Wait, why is he including my items with his? As if he was reading my mind, he turns towards me.

"Are you okay with sharing?"

I never share a fitting room with anyone except Leah, but we're best friends, so I don't find that awkward. But sharing with Reece, who's a guy, also doesn't seem awkward, which is quite surprising. What's the worst that can happen? I mean, it's not like he's into me; we're just two friends sharing a space with limited movement.

"Yeah, that would be fine," I assure him.

The associate informs us that we can only take ten items in at a time. The lights in the fitting room are bright.

"I can use the mirror on the left, if you want to take the one on the right," Reece suggests.

I nod in agreement. Although I didn't pick up as many items as he and Leah, I did manage to find a couple pairs of pants while they were discussing fashion. *Whoa, he's removing his shirt. Okay, turn around. Focus on getting out as soon as possible.* I take off the khaki shorts I have on and pull on a pair of jeans. I wouldn't normally wear jeans with a slit over the knee, but these light-blue jeans look cool.

"You should get those jeans; they fit nicely."

I look up, seeing he's smiling at me in the mirror. He's putting on a shirt and I notice the left side of his chest is uncovered.

"Thanks, I'm glad you think so."

I look back up to see his eyes looking still into mine. I begin rummaging through the clothes I collected. Okay, maybe this isn't so bad. It's not like he's staring. Obviously, my paranoia is getting the best of me. As soon as I remove my shorts and try on jeans, a sigh of frustration fills the room. I look up in the mirror and notice he's having difficulty buttoning the shirt.

"Would you like some help?"

He looks embarrassed. I can't even count how many times Leah has helped me with the button on numerous shirts.

"Could you?" He almost looks lost.

I walk over to inspect his shirt and notice he skipped a button towards the bottom.

"Well, first, we need to correct this guy."

I point at the bottom of his shirt. I attempt to reach for it and he grabs my wrist. I look into his eyes swallowing a big gulp as he stares at me in silence.

"Is something wrong?" I ask.

"You seem flustered."

Maybe if you let go, I wouldn't be.

"No, I'm ok," I assure him.

He releases his grip and I proceed with unbuttoning the shirt from the bottom, working my way up. I find myself staring into those beautiful grey eyes of his. Once I finally reach the top button, I adjust the shirt to align it properly.

"What do you think about this color?"

I analyze the grey plaid. Well, it goes perfectly well with his eyes. He stretches his back, causing the shirt to open and reveal more of his body. I turn my head towards the mirror.

"I think it's nice."

He follows my gaze and stares at me in the mirror's reflection.

"Wouldn't it be better if you actually looked?"

I turn my face back towards him.

"I think it fits you well."

He grins and I continue buttoning the shirt. After the last one, he pulls out a bowtie.

"Can you help me with this?"

I'm a pro at fixing ties, but not bowties. After a few awkward attempts between us, we are finally able to make it look presentable.

"That wasn't so bad. What do you think?"

He looks at himself in the mirror and says, "I couldn't have asked for anything better."

Well, I'm glad he's in a good mood; now I can finish trying on some more looks. I put on some dress pants, and each item from the pile of pastels Leah picked out, and then a black short-sleeve button-down shirt. I also try on a grey bowtie with white polka dots.

"Do you mind?" I signal for Reece for some assistance. He shifts his attention to me and I can't help but notice the scent he's wearing. It's the same cologne I use. I wonder how long he's been a fan. "I like your fragrance; I've been using the same one for about five years now." I can tell he's focused on fixing the bowtie fix due to his lack of response. "So, I bet you wouldn't want to go shopping with Leah again." I laugh.

He stops and looks at me right in the eyes. Staring into his eyes is mesmerizing. He's a beautiful guy. *Wait, did I just call this guy beautiful. What's happening here?*

"Do you always get this nervous when someone's close to you?" he asks.

Well, no one except Leah has been this close to me; what do you think? I mean, come on, I barely know you, and here we are, sharing a fitting room and seeing each other half-naked. Who wouldn't be a bit uncomfortable in this setting?

"Who's nervous? I'm just making conversation."

He places his hands on my shoulders, giving me a firm squeeze. I'm not sure if that was an assurance squeeze or *Get it together, man.*

"Is this your first time, lad?"

I stare, confused at the question. He laughs and releases my shoulders, stepping back.

"Sharing a fitting room with a bloke?"

I look at the mirror, checking out the bowtie.

"It's not every day I share a fitting room with someone."

He smiles and changes into some black pants.

Looking at my image, I try my best at sounding casual and say, "This looks nice; I wouldn't mind wearing this to a nice dinner."

Reece continues to analyze his outfit and then mine.

"I agree; where should we go tonight?"

I wasn't expecting to do anything with him after this, especially with everything that's going on with Leah and Anthony. Maybe she might enjoy eating out with us.

"I don't know, but once we finish up here, maybe the three of us could decide on something together."

He smirks and shakes his head. What was that look about?

After spending thirty minutes in the fitting room with Reece, he and I manage to put back half of the items we had. Leah, of course, was outside waiting for us.

"Well, I'm glad you both decided on something." She surveys both of our choices. "Eww." We both laugh at her succinct thoughts regarding the cut-up jeans in Reece's hand.

"Awe, bow-ties; how cute." She rolls her eyes and wanders off.

I roll my eyes and follow her.

"Did you find anything?" I ask.

She turns around with an annoyed look.

"No Cam, I didn't; otherwise, my hands would be full." She walks off.

Okay, someone has an issue she would like to address. I get that she's upset about this whole situation with Anthony, but she shouldn't lash out at me.

I run after Leah and jump in front of her before she reaches the counter.

"Time out. Leah, I get that you're scared and confused, but the reason we came here was to help you clear your mind; not get stressed out and argumentative."

She sighs and wraps her arms around me.

"I know, you're right; I'm sorry, I just don't know what to do."

Smiling in defeat, I instantly soften when she hugs me.

"Reece invited us to dinner."

She pushes me away and punches me in the shoulder.

"Did he invite just you or *us*?"

I glare at her.

"Well?" she asks impatiently.

Why does it matter?

"I mentioned something about dinner based on my outfit choice, and he asked where we should go," I reply while rubbing my shoulder. "And I said between the three of us, we could decide."

She raises a fist, preparing to punch. I close my eyes and brace myself, waiting for impact. After a few seconds, when the blow doesn't come, I peek and Leah is staring at me, grinning from ear to ear. What's her deal? She was just about to let me have it, but now she seems happy.

"My dear sweet Cameron, you were asked on a date, and you felt the need to include me."

She slaps the arm she punched moments before. I groan on the inside.

"Maybe it'll be a nice, fancy restaurant," she says, "but then again, it could be fast food. If that's the case, you should cancel." She pulls out her phone and starts typing.

Why is it that out of every human being I've ever met, she and I became best friends? It's a question I have yet to answer, but who cares? I love her, and that's what matters.

"That's not what I said or what's happening," I retort.

She backs away with her arms up. "Why so sensitive Cam? I'm simply acknowledging what you said." She reaches over and grabs the shirt and pants in my hands and walks up to the cashier. "My treat." She hands the cashier her card.

HELLO PLAN

The drive back with Leah was full of back-and-forth discussions about Reece and me. She doesn't think two guys can be around each other in a fitting room and call themselves just friends.

"What two guys do you know share a fitting room?"

"Leah what's wrong with sharing a fitting room?"

"Cameron! A guy wants to be alone with you in a fitting room and you don't see the issue?"

No matter what I say, she's going to find a counter-response. I've learned that ignoring Leah will eventually get her to listen.

"Well?"

I find it quite amusing that she's so passionate about a conversation that has more to do with her perspective. It's like talking to yourself in the mirror. You say what you think might make you feel better.

"Cam, are you listening to anything I'm saying?" I give her a smirk and turn up the music.

"Fine, I'll drop it." She leans back in her seat.

I turn the volume lower. "So, how are you feeling?" I ask.

After a few seconds, she responds. "Honestly, I don't know what to feel." She sighs and looks out the window.

It pains me to see her so sad. This situation between her and Anthony needs a resolution soon. I know I shouldn't get involved, but I want to help. The question is, what should I do? I could call Anthony and tell him everything, but I don't want to break Leah's trust and create a rift. But whenever Leah and I get into a big fight, usually one of us apologizes the same day. If I could just get her and Anthony in a room long enough to talk things out… I could invite him over one day, then just casually have Leah come by. Once she arrived, I could play it off. There's no way she should get mad; it would be harmless. That doesn't seem too obvious. After all, it's not like he's a stranger to me. There's no way she would suspect my involvement then. That's it, that's what I should do. I can text Anthony later tonight and create a casual conversation. After all, he and I have a bond outside of his and Leah's relationship. I glance over at Leah, and she's still staring out the window.

That's when I notice a tear rolling down her cheeks.

"You're amazing; you know that," I say to her. She turns towards me.

"I think that in the end, you will do what's right." I reassure her by squeezing her hand.

She tightens her grip, then turns back towards the window.

"I love you Cam."

I glance over again, and her eyes are closed.

"I love you too Leah."

Once we're inside, Leah goes into my bedroom. I can tell she's exhausted. I follow behind.

"I'll be in the living room if you need me."

She raises her hand in bed, giving me the thumbs up. I pull out my phone due to alert notifications. Some of the messages are pictures of Riley and her friend. It looks like nacho night was fun; I respond with "looks tasty." The other texts are from Reece. He wants to know if Italian food would be okay. I respond with a thumbs-up emoji. Now that Leah's resting, I can use this opportunity to reach out to Anthony. I figure it would be better to call than text, so I sneak into the hallway just in case Leah decides to get up for any reason. After four rings, he answers.

"Hi Anthony, how are you?"

Of course he's not great; his girlfriend just dumped him without much of an explanation. *Just remember Cam, don't jump the gun and mention the pregnancy.* It's bad enough to call him when my best friend told me to stay out of it. What she doesn't know won't hurt, right?

"I'm just trying to figure things out. Have you spoken with Leah? he asks.

"Yeah, she's okay, just resting at the moment."

The worry in his voice has sent me into panic mode. He cares for her and wants to be with her. I stifle the impulse to yell out that she's pregnant and confused; again, it's not my place. But Anthony's different from the other guys Leah dated, and it's awful knowing how much he's hurting.

He's thoughtful, warm, and funny. Oh man, this is going to be more complicated than I thought.

"She's there? Really? I'm heading over."

"No! you shouldn't come over now; she's still upset."

Leah can't know I called him. If he drives over here now, it'll come out that I called. I mean, it's not crazy that she's at my apartment. Anytime Leah or I get upset about anything we usually go over to each other's place and just sit around talking about our feelings. Sometimes we just lie there in silence, holding each other's hands. Anthony witnessed us lying in bed before; after a long talk and a lot of him drinking, he accepted our friendship.

"Anthony, just stay put. I'll let you know if anything changes, okay?"

"Okay, I'll try to be patient and trust that things will work out."

"I'm sure they will. Take care Anthony."

After we hang up, a tear falls down my right cheek. He really loves her. There's no way I can let this go on for much longer. Either she's going to have to woman-up, or I'll have to act. It seems like I'll have to rule out the "coincidental" meeting between the two. *Think, Cameron; what else can you do?*

17

HELLO CURIOSITY

Reece and I end up at Sterling's, a popular restaurant in Rochester. The free mozzarella cheese sticks here are amazing; I've eaten a total of five so far. We're both wearing the outfits we purchased earlier today. The setting here is very nice; tea lights floating in glasses and white roses are the centerpiece. I like how the stems on the flowers are cut low, so you can enjoy your meal while still making eye contact. My phone keeps dinging with messages from Leah. She wants photos of the place and is curious about what I'm eating. She and I have discussed coming here for months.

"Is everything alright?"

I can tell Reece is worried.

I might be concerned too if his phone kept going off every few minutes.

"Sorry. It's fine. Leah says hello."

Okay, time to put you on silent. But before turning off the sound, I see one more alert with an emoji that has a wink.

"What's the verdict?" he asks.

"Well, Leah and Anthony are still trying to figure things out. I promised her I wouldn't get involved, but it's hard not to." I place my phone in my back pocket, waiting for him to respond.

"Well, that is a worry. I do hope they work it out, but I was actually talking about those." He points towards the cheesy appetizers. "There's only so much you can do for people and their own problems; try not to get so worked up, Cameron." He grabs a mozzarella stick.

I'm so focused on their issue instead of what's happening now.

"I'm sorry," I respond.

"It's fine… wins and losses happen daily." He waves his hand. "True. Make sure you remember that once you're defeated…" Reece raises an eyebrow.

"…in Laser Tag that is."

Judging by the smirk on his face, he's quite amused by my statement. Sure he's fit, and can run and climb rocks, but I have instincts. A strong mentality is just as good as a strong physicality, if not better.

"You're so confident, Sir Cam."

Hmm, that's new. "Sir Cam." It does have an excellent sound to it. Wait, are we close enough for him to call me Cam?

"However, I'm still undefeated." He steps forward and looks me straight in the eyes, waiting for a response.

I could try to say something witty, but he would probably only provide a more comical response. Instead, I choose to simply stuff my face with another free mozzarella stick.

"How are things with you and Riley?" he asks.

"She's doing well. We plan to grab frozen yogurt before you and I hit the Laser Tag place."

Speaking of her, I probably should check in, but then again, I don't want to come off as clingy.

The waiter returns with a glass pitcher of water and hands us menus.

"Hi, my name's Andre; I'll be your waiter. I'll give you time to go over the menu."

Looking at the menu, I see that the prices here are fair. That's a plus. Ooh, they have spinach dip with pita chips. Oh, wow, they have linguine pasta with garlic sauce, lemon, parmesan, roasted red peppers, and shrimp. I think I've found my entrée.

"What do you fancy about Riley?"

Well, there are so many things I could say. I mean, she's funny, outgoing, gorgeous. I could go on and on, but the one thing that comes to mind is…

"She's different. I've never met a girl who's that direct and goes for what she wants."

I look into his eyes and they look blue. I'd been sure they were grey, but maybe it's the lighting causing them to look blue.

"Your eyes…"

"They change color. It happens quite often, mostly due to lighting."

That's awesome. I wonder if he gets a lot of compliments on his eyes. He probably does; just another thing probably making the girls and guys throw themselves at him. I, on the other hand, don't have that problem. Hopefully, time with Riley will change that. In the meantime, I'll continue to work on my friendship with Reece.

"Have you both decided on anything?" Andre has appeared. "Perhaps some drinks?"

There's so much to choose from here. The raspberry lemon tea sounds good, as well as the Hibiscus tea.

"What are your thoughts on the teas?" I ask.

He takes a moment to think. He seems very organized, order pads in one side of the apron pocket and pens and straws in the other. I never really understood why pens and straws are in the apron pocket. I guess it appears more manageable than having to wonder whether they have enough when the drinks come.

"I like the lemon honey flavor or the butterfly lemonade."

I didn't think to check out the lemonades; there is a total of five flavors.

"The lemonade sounds tasty; I'll try the butterfly one. Could I also get the spinach dip with pita chips?"

He nods his head and starts writing down the request.

"I'll also have the lemonade; we'll share the dip," Reece responds.

It's almost like he read my mind. Sharing this dip is so much better than letting go to waste what I can't eat.

"Have you decided on entrees?" Andre asks.

I want pasta, but I feel like I should try something different. However, the one I was reading the description about was mouthwatering.

"I'll have the ribeye steak with mashed potatoes and mac and cheese," Reece says with a smile.

Andre smiles back at Reece nervously. They share a gaze for a moment. Well, there's clearly some attraction here. I clear my throat, and they both look at me.

"I'll have the linguine pasta."

"Very well. I'll get this food order in and be right back with your drinks." While grabbing the menus, the waiter steals another glance at Reece.

After fifteen minutes of laughing and chatting, our spinach dip arrives. Reece is the first to dig in and goes on about how delicious it is.

"If you could be any animal, what would you be?" he asks.

A little strange, hmm, but let's see. What animal? There are so many, and each one has its perks.

"I would say a hawk."

He gazes into my eyes for a moment.

"You don't agree with my choice?"

He continues to stare. I lean forward, waiting for him to respond.

"I can see it," he murmurs finally. "It may just be your spirit animal."

I've heard about people taking tests for their spirit animals. I have yet to try. He pulls out his phone and starts typing. I continue eating more dip.

"According to this website," he says, "hawks have an open perspective on situations."

Whoa, maybe he's right. I don't limit myself to one option, and I'd considered myself open-minded.

"Nice to know. What would your spirit animal be?"

He leans back and thinks for a bit.

"An owl. I can see what others can't." An owl? Not sure that would've been one I'd used to describe him.

Andre returns with our plates.

"Alright, gentlemen, here are your entrees; I hope you both enjoy."

After dinner, Reece asks if we can take a photo outside the building. He says this is a moment he wants to treasure. I think it's fascinating that he and I have developed such a close bond so quickly.

"Thanks for dinner, I enjoyed it," I offer.

He stares at me without responding. What could he possibly be thinking?

"I did too. Thanks for coming out with me."

After a few more glances and looking around, we hug each other, part, and wave goodbye.

After making it back to my apartment, I find Leah lying on the sofa all covered up.

"Finally." She sits up and turns off the television. "How was it?"

She seems eager to know how dinner with Reece went. However, I'm more interested in what she's been doing since I've been gone.

"Not much happened… Have you spoken with Anthony?"

She throws the cover off and walks up to me. "What does 'not much' mean?"

Ugh, she's deflecting.

"We talked and ate some food. What else was going to happen?" I plop down onto the sofa.

"You talked?" Leah over-enunciates while folding her arms.

I pull out my phone and she snatches it to apparently keep me on topic.

"What the…"

"Talked about what exactly?" she demands.

I run my fingers over my face. "Nothing in particular, just normal conversation. If there was something I thought you should know I would tell you."

She stands there just looking at me. Is she even blinking?

"Now can you please hand me back my phone and answer *my* question?"

She tosses the phone at me and says, "I'm meeting Anthony on Friday."

Friday? The same day I'll be spending time with Riley and Reece? Just great, this is going to be the most crucial conversation she could have. I want to be there for any fallout, but it happens to be on the one day I have plans with this amazing woman… and this great new friend.

"Is it possible for you to do it sooner?" I ask.

She rolls her eyes in frustration and slumps onto the couch. "Look, I know you made arrangements, and I want you to keep those plans." She grabs my hand. "This is something I have to do on my own, and it's important to me that you don't worry." She places a hand on my cheek.

"I love you Cam, and I thank you for everything you've done and continue to do."

"Okay, but if anything goes wrong, just get a hold of me immediately. I want to be there for you."

"I promise."

She embraces me in a tight hug, and we sit there, holding each other for the rest of the night.

HELLO DUTY
Tuesday

After a late night with Leah, I've come to accept that I'm unable to save her from every obstacle. As much as I want to protect her, I must learn to let her fight her own battles. By the time we both got to that understanding, it was 2 AM, so here I am just a few hours later, exhausted and about to start work. Before my shift starts, though, my partner Jessie and I decide to grab breakfast at Justine's, a place known for its amazing bagels. My favorite is the asiago cheese variety with some chive cream cheese. Jessie is feeling fruit-forward today and gets the blueberry with raspberry cream cheese. We wait about ten minutes before our order is ready.

"You didn't come in yesterday; everything okay, Cameron?"

Jessie and I have worked together for the past three months. We talk about all sorts of things, but we don't typically discuss any personal problems at work.

"Things are better; I just had some stuff to take care of. How's the wife?" Jessie and his wife Amber are expecting their firstborn.

"She's due any day now, and she's on bed rest." They were trying to get pregnant the first year in the marriage but were unsuccessful. Then on Valentine's Day, they found out they were going to have a baby. "Speaking of, I better check in and see how's she's doing."

He walks off towards the van with his order and I stay inside to eat my bagel while it's still warm. Twenty minutes later, he returns and asks if I'm ready to go. Judging by the cream cheese on the side of his mouth, I assume he is.

Our first stop was for a grandpa who had a stroke. Luckily two teenage grandchildren were there and able to call for help. After we transported him to the hospital, we received a call for a young girl who passed out due to dehydration. This morning had its ups and downs, but we managed. Four hours into our shift, and I'm already exhausted. But it's time for lunch. We end up at some local sandwich shop. A familiar voice is placing a large order.

"Riley?"

She turns around and gives me the biggest smile. "Cameron, what are you doing on this side of town?"

I like the sound of my name coming from her mouth.

"My partner and I are on our lunch break," I respond.

"Same here, just grabbing food for the ladies at the shop."

"So, is it safe to say that the ladies are mechanics as well?"

She laughs and gives me a push. "Yes, my shop is staffed only by women."

Whoa, I didn't know she owned the shop. What else don't I know about you?

"Are we still on for Friday, Cameron?"

She looks gorgeous in her uniform. Olive is a pretty color on her. It brings out her eyes.

"Hello… Cameron, are you there?"

Startled by her waving her hands in front of my face, I jump.

"Oh yeah, can't wait."

We embrace. She smells like shea butter.

"Alright, well, I'm heading over to the pick-up line; see you soon."

I order a veggie sandwich and some baked chips with a bottle of water. Jessie orders the Philly cheesesteak and BBQ chips with a Sprite. Our lunch break is an hour and we spend most of it talking about Riley. He watched our interaction and asked what was taking so long for us to make it official. I explained how we met and how long it's been. We then talk more about his wife, the baby, and the nursery.

"Hey Cam, would you mind helping me put together the crib?"

Anyone that knows me knows I'm not the handy type.

"Um, okay. When were you thinking of doing this?"

"I'll get back to you on the date."

For the most part, after lunchtime, our shift goes by quicker than I thought it would. We have a couple of calls, but luckily it isn't too bad. I've had some rough ones during my time out in the field; domestic abuse, big fires, multiple car pile-ups, but in the end we manage to save the day a lot of the time. But there are also a number of not-so-lucky instances, and some have taken a toll on me. Five o'clock arrives, and I am ready to clock out.

"Cam, wait up," Jessie yells.

He's running towards me as I turn around.

"So what about Thursday; could you help me put the nursery together then?"

"Sure, that would be okay."

"Thanks bud, you have no idea how many times I've tried putting this thing together alone."

If he was unable to do it after many failed attempts, I guess a few more from me won't hurt. Leah and I have texted numerous times throughout the day. She also went back to work. She mentioned she and Anthony were keeping their distance until Friday. It must pain them both to see each other at work at the hospital, knowing their relationship is suffering. I sent her silly pics, hoping to distract her.

Tonight, I figure I'll watch a movie or something on TV to pass some time. Not much catches my attention except some reruns of classic shows. By the time I find something to watch, I start drifting off. I'm not going to be able to make it through an entire episode. Then the ringing of my phone wakes me up. It's Leah crying on the line.

"Cam, I'm so frustrated with my coworkers."

"Leah, calm down, what happened?"

"Why are they so focused on what he and I have going on?"

It was only a matter of time before the whole hospital knew about her and Anthony. Their lack of contact was probably very noticeable, not to mention body language—no way to hide that. "Don't stress yourself out about what others think" She sniffles on the line.

"Only you and Anthony should be concerned about the status of your relationship; don't focus on others' opinions."

"You're right. It just sucks though, you know?" She sniffles again. "I already have so much to deal with, between the break-up, gossip, and visits back and forth with my mom; it's becoming really draining." She starts to sob now.

"I can take your mom to her next doctor's appointment. When is it?"

"No, this is something I have to do… thanks to my dad."

Her dad left her mother while she was sick. He said they were having problems before, and that he couldn't handle all the stress. I'm no expert on marriage, but when you've been with someone for twenty-five years, you don't just up and leave. There wasn't any counseling; he just decided he wanted out. What jerk would leave his family in their time of need? Now, Leah works long hours and has to pay for someone to watch her mother. I've been able to help when I'm not on call and have also been slipping her some money. When I hang out with her mother, we usually play games, watch movies, listen to music, and even dance sometimes when she's feeling up to it. Still, I'm no substitute. A man should not leave his family; he should protect them no matter what. I don't like divorce; I never have. Trust me, I understand things can be complex, but you should start by taking a step back and breathing. It saddens me to know that couples invest so much time together and, within any moment, could give up.

"How about I at least pick up the medicine?" I offer.

"I'll get that once I get off work, but thanks, Cam."

"You're welcome."

Silence lingers on the line.

"Well, let me finish up, I'm about to head out soon, talk to you later. Love you."

"Love you, too."

There's a knock at the door. I wasn't expecting anyone.

"Who is it?"

I hear a muffled voice on the other side. Either they speak softly, or the wood is pretty thick.

I walk over and look out the peep hole, and to my surprise, it's her.

HELLO FEELINGS

"Well, aren't you going to invite me in?" Riley asks, standing in the hallway.

I wasn't expecting to see her twice in a day, yet here she is, standing in her uniform with some take-out bags. Judging by the smell, she brought Chinese takeout.

"Of course, come in."

After placing the bags on the table, she goes to the couch and sits down. I follow her. We sit there a few seconds just staring and smiling at each other.

"So…what prompts this visit?"

She stands back up and walks back and forth a bit before she speaks.

"Mercedes and I fought."

Leah and I have had many disagreements while living together. It's normal for roommates to have those at some point. But what advice do I give her when I really don't know much about her or Mercedes.

"What exactly happened?" I ask.

"Anytime she visits my job, there's a conflict with her and my employees. If she sees me laughing or just being vaguely friendly with a colleague, she starts causing trouble."

To me, that sounds like a jealous friend. Why would you not be okay with your friend making other friends? It's a part of being human; you meet others and sometimes develop a bond.

"What are the conflicts about?"

"The relationships I have with them," Riley says sitting back down.

"Maybe she's afraid of you getting closer to someone else."

Close friends like being around each other as much as they can, and some friends are just clingier than others. It doesn't mean it's a bad thing. The friends just might require more attention. *I* would like to spend more time with Riley, but I understand she has other friends and I respect that.

She stares into my eyes. In that moment, I feel we are connected. I'm not sure how to explain it, but it's almost like we're seeing each other for the first time. I wonder if she feels the same way. I doubt it; she hasn't given me any reason to let me know she's interested, other than asking me out, but anyone could invite someone out. Maybe I'm not her type. Often, I get placed in the friend zone. There was this girl Rachel who said I was too nice. Then there was Morgan. She ghosted me without any explanation. Oh, and Tiffany flat out said she only wanted to be friends because she didn't feel "that excited." I guess that's another way of saying I was boring to her.

"Should we eat? What did you bri—"

Riley leans in and kisses me. I can't help myself and return the kiss. This was a moment I didn't think would happen for some time, but I'm glad it is. Her lips are soft, also sweet. I'm assuming that's bubblegum-flavored lip gloss I'm tasting. She grabs the back of my head, pulling me closer to her. I start to do the same, but she pushes me back. My heart is racing. She presses her lips against mine once more and this one lasts about a minute with my fingers tangled in her hair. Then she pulls back.

"Riley, what's wrong?"

She gets up quickly and fixes her hair.

Oh no, does she think I'm a terrible kisser? Did she not enjoy it? Maybe it was too much and too fast. She starts looking in the couch cushions. I call her name, but she ignores me.

"Where are my keys?" she asks.

I get up, helping her to look.

"I can't find them; I have to go."

She's clearly starting to panic. I try to reach for her, but she pushes me away.

"Found them. I'm so sorry, Cameron, but I have to go."

I move to calm her down; I don't want her to leave like this.

"Riley, please stay. Can we talk?"

She shakes her head no and runs out of the apartment. I follow her into the hallway.

"Did I do something wrong?"

She runs faster until she gets to the elevator. She spins around.

"Look, you did nothing wrong; it was all me. I shouldn't have done that. You and I won't work." The elevator opens, and she steps inside.

Before the doors close, she turns to me and says, "Goodbye, Cameron."

HELLO AWKWARDNESS
Wednesday

"Give me her number now," Leah demands.

I had explained to her what all took place last night with Riley, so she and I decide to meet up after work at her home. I knew she would overreact, but I didn't realize to what extent.

"Why, it's not going to change anything?" I plead.

She grabs her keys from the counter and walks back over to me.

"Get up; we're going to her work."

That's insane; there's no way I'm causing a scene, especially at someone's place of business. Besides I'm not even sure where she works. I sit there with my arms folded; I'll wait for her to cool off.

"So you want me to go over there alone?"

Of course not; I can't afford to have my pregnant best friend in jail because she decided that assaulting someone who's giving me seriously mixed romantic signals was okay.

"I have no idea where she works, so how do *you* expect to find her?"

Annoyed, she walks closer to me and bends over until we're eye to eye.

"I guess we'll be driving to every mechanic shop," she yells. "Go get your ass to the car, Cameron!"

There's no way this is healthy: newly pregnant *and* angry.

Why did I have to share my hurt feelings with someone who's already hurting? *Not cool, not cool at all.*

"Leah, please just take a moment and breathe."

She stands straight up and lets out a deep breath. But then she throws her keys.

Pregnancy is bringing out her dark side, and it hasn't even been a whole month.

"I see what you're up to, and it's not going to work," she retorts.

If that's the case, then you should know it's to help you.

"Leah, we've just been on one date and hung out a little. And anyway, maybe there's more to why she reacted that way."

Leah glares at me for a few seconds, but then the hardness in her eyes softens a little. "Fine, I won't interfere since you promised not to interfere with Anthony and me."

If only that were true. I spoke to Anthony on the phone during my drive here. He seemed to be more upset since we last spoke. During our conversation, I may have let it slip that Leah had something significant to tell him. He was so anxious to know what it was, but I assured him it wasn't bad, and he couldn't ask her about it until she brought it up. If Leah knew, I don't know what she would do.

"Exactly," I reply, not quite looking her in the eye. "So please respect my situation and let it be."

I feel horrible and guilty. And Leah knows me too well; she would see it in my face, so I quickly get up to grab a cranberry juice in her kitchen. I should've never inserted myself. She trusts me, and I broke that trust going behind her back. I pull out my phone and see that Reece has texted asking about my plans for tomorrow. I mention how after work I have to figure out how to put together a crib and a nursery. He mentions he has a few ideas that might help and asks if he could tag along. He is very eager to help. Or maybe he's eager to see me. Whatever the situation, I text that I'll get back him if that's cool with my friend.

"Is that the Irishman?"

I jump at the sound of Leah's voice. "He has a name."

She rolls her eyes and grabs my cranberry juice to take a sip. "Whatever. Was that him?" She hands it back.

I nod my head yes.

"What does he want?"

"He wants to know if he could help me with Jessie and Amber's nursery."

I place my phone back in my pocket and take a sip of the cranberry juice. Now let's wait and hear the silliness that's about to come out of her mouth.

"And you said yes?"

I walk around the counter to the dining room table and sit in a chair. The black and gold decorations she has in this room make for a good combination of colors. I remember when we first moved out here and went shopping for new places two years ago. We were both so excited about this next chapter in our lives. I don't think either of us expected the expenses to be as high as they were, sharing an apartment together the first six months helped us both save a bit.

I receive another alert on my phone; to my surprise, it's Riley. She's asking if I would meet her at her place. Part of me wants to say, "No, leave me alone." However, the other part of me wants to know what's going on. Why did she react the way she did? It's not like I initiated the kiss.

"It's Riley; she wants to meet up."

Leah starts inhaling and exhaling slowly. She walks over and snatches the phone out of my hands.

"What are you doing?!" I ask, panicked.

She starts typing, I immediately get up and try to grab back the phone, but she's too quick.

She runs into the restroom and locks the door.

"Leah, this is not okay. What are you saying to her?"

Not one noise comes from the other side of the door.

"Leah."

I knock on the door, and still no response. Not good; she's pissed, and taking her frustration out on Riley, which will not help our situation. I knock harder, desperately hoping she'll come out.

"Will you stop before you break the door?" she yells on the other side.

I continue to knock until finally she opens the door and shoves the phone in my chest. I open up my messages to see what was said, but they're gone.

"Why did you delete the messages?"

She ignores me and sits on the couch in the living room.

"What did you say?" Still no response.

"You had no right…" I say, my voice starting to rise, but before I can finish my sentence, she throws a pillow at me.

"Just shut up. You'll find out when you get there."

"Tell me now!" I demand.

She turns on the TV. Instead of questioning her further, I grab my keys and head for the door; I figure I should leave before saying something I'll regret.

"Where are you going?"

I slam the door on my way out to my car. I'm so upset with her; how does she not see the problem? It's wrong for me to intervene, but not for her? Yeah, I know we're not a couple, but still. I get it; I have no right to be upset when I've had multiple conversations with Anthony behind her back, but she doesn't *know* that. My phone starts ringing, and I see Leah's name appear on caller ID. I ignore the call, the phone rings again, and I press to decline. I need time to cool off; answering my phone right now would only upset me more. I'd start yelling, then she'll start screaming, and it'll just create this big drama ending with us not speaking to each other. I don't want that; I still care about her, and she needs me no matter how upset I am. She calls again, and I just let the phone ring. Once I make it to my car, I receive a text from Jessie about the time tomorrow. I assure him I'll be there and ask if bringing a friend would be okay; he says yes. My phone rings again, and this time it's from Riley. Do I answer or ignore? Ugh, what if she starts yelling at me? I let the phone go to voicemail.

Whatever she wants to say to me, she can say in person.

21

HELLO REASON

Forty-five minutes later, I make it to Riley's place; she texted me the address as I was sitting outside Leah's apartment. Had I known she was this far away, I would've asked her to meet me somewhere local. I mean, driving over forty minutes for someone to tell you they don't want to see you again is a waste of time; this could've been a phone conversation.

When I pull up to her place, she's standing outside waiting for me. I guess she doesn't want any drama inside her home. But once I exit my car, she hugs me. What's going on here?

"How was the drive?" she asks.

It was long, quiet, annoying, upsetting, what do you think?

"It was okay," I respond.

My complaining will only make this situation more awkward. I follow her into her building; she lives on the third floor. Her apartment complex is big. From what I could see on the sign, there are several buildings, hers being number fifteen. We go inside her place and it smells like sandalwood. She has a lot of tools piled up in the corner. Her bar area is spacious. Judging by the multiple bottles on the shelves, she likes her wine. She gestures for me to sit on the couch.

Riley is nervous; she's pacing back and forth. She's obviously trying to figure out how to break it to me. I get it; you're not into me—you made that clear. Why don't you say whatever is on your mind now? It'll hurt but, at least her saying it out loud makes it real and I can move on.

"If this was too soon…" I start to say.

She raises her hand, signaling for me to stay quiet. I sit there with folded arms, waiting for her to speak.

"I want to apologize to you for yesterday."

Great, she finally opens her mouth; there's the apology, so what's next? Are you going to offer up the classic, "It's not you, it's me? But oh, we can still be friends"?

"You deserve an explanation."

Of course I do. You kissed me, then left as if I did something wrong. Did you ever think about how that would make me feel? No, of course you didn't.

"Mercedes and I fought."

Okay, tell me something you haven't already said.

"It was about you." She looks up, and judging by her face, she is waiting for a reaction.

Instead, I sit there quietly with my arms folded. I could overreact, but what good would that do? I'm not sure what their disagreement had to do with me. It's not like Mercedes and I have gotten to know each other.

"She's not okay with us making plans and excluding her."

Our plans have nothing to do with her; she's a friend and should understand that not everything is about her. Me taking Riley out or inviting her anywhere doesn't have to include her.

Mercedes should be happy that her friend found someone interested in her or someone she likes.

"Riley, have you tried talking with Mercedes?"

She takes a seat next to me and covers her face. Is that a no? She shifts further back into the sofa. Okay, maybe it's time for me to go. I begin to stand up only to get pulled back down. Based on her expression, I can tell she's hurting. The question is, why? Why do you have to let someone else's feelings overpower your own? Say whatever it is you want to say.

"I have, and it led to a bigger argument."

It sounds like Mercedes may be controlling.

"Look Riley, it seems like you have some things to figure out on your own." I stand up once more. She seems more concerned about her relationship with Mercedes than ours. At this point I'm unsure of what to classify us as. Are we dating or are we just friends? Does she like me romantically or not? This is confusing and I don't want to continue stressing about something that doesn't seem as important to her. I make my way to the door.

"Will you stay here tonight?" she asks.

I wasn't expecting that. I assumed we'd have a conversation; she'd tell me whatever we've been building has to end, and that would be that. Instead, she wants to have a sleepover? I would like to, but what if Mercedes comes back and has a tantrum? Would Riley kick me out because she didn't ask for permission to have a guest?

"I came here for answers, and that doesn't seem like something you can give me now."

She walks over and grabs both my hands.

"You were right," she says softly.

Right? What was I right about?

"After some thinking, reading your text made sense, I can see why you may view me as selfish and manipulative."

When did I… wait the text Leah sent from my phone.

"Riley, that wasn't what I…"

She leans in and kisses me. This time it's tender.

"Will you stay the night?"

"Do you think that's a good idea?"

She walks into the hallway, signaling me to follow. She grabs my hand with a firm grip and looks up, and smiles.

"There's no one else I would want to stay the night." She wraps her arms around me. This feels nice; I would like to have more moments like this with her, but will it last? I return the hug, and we just stand there soaking in every minute of it.

"So…?" she asks hesitantly.

Okay, Cameron, will you stay or go? Let's weigh the pros and cons. If I stay, we spend more time together and maybe I'll get a chance to know her better; her likes, dislikes, or more about her family and friends. There are also dreams and aspirations I want to find out about. Oh, and you can't forget about pet peeves. But if I go, I may resent it later; we may never speak again, she'll say something hurtful, or maybe I will. Mercedes might… no stop, this isn't about Mercedes; this is the moment for Riley and me to grow.

"Of course," I respond while resting my chin on her head. Will tonight be the beginning of us? We let this development sit there comfortably for a few seconds.

"So have you eaten anything?"

I shake my head no. She pulls away from the hug, but grabs me to make our way to her kitchen. I take a seat at near the counter. Based on the spinach and kale she's pulling out of the Refrigerator, I assume she's about to make a salad.

"I'll add salmon; that way, we'll have our protein."

I watch as she cuts the salmon into chunks. She then seasons them and heats some oil in a pan on the stove.

"How long have you known Mercedes?"

She adds the chopped salmon into the skillet.

"Five years."

"Where did you meet?"

"On campus."

She places her hand in my hair and runs her fingers through it. I take a huge swallow, a little nervous at the intimacy.

"You have soft hair."

"Thank you."

"How long have you known Leah?"

"Since we were kids."

She removes her hand to start stirring the salmon.

"Have you ever had a crush on her?" she asks without looking at me and grinning.

"No! Never," I shriek. Quickly re-pitching my voice lower, I change the subject. "So, what do you have planned for us to do?"

She signals me with her finger to come in closer. "The best part about spending time together is not having a plan."

I laugh, but she reads the confusion on my face.

"Well, if you must know, I figured we'd just eat, talk, and maybe watch some movies."

Okay, not bad. That's a typical night to have.

"Let's just enjoy the moment," she says.

After a couple of hours of talking, we decide to go for a walk at the park. It's cool outside. Riley and I stroll around in silence holding hands. I look over to see her head down, wearing a slight grin.

Looking straight ahead, I ask, "What are you thinking?"

"How lucky I am."

I can't help but smile. I close the gap between us as we continue walking.

"*I'm* the lucky one."

She lifts her head towards me; her eyes begin to look glossy. "What are you most afraid of?" she asks.

Afraid of? Hmmm, definitely flying and cruises or anything else that doesn't involve me being on solid land.

"I would say mostly planes."

She lets go of my hand as I take another step forward. I turn to face her.

"Planes?" she scoffs.

"With valid reasons."

She folds her arms while staring at me.

"What about you?"

"Not planes." She nudges me with her shoulder and keeps walking.

"Well, you continue to fly while I drive," I call after her.

We reach a bench and she takes a seat. She looks over, signaling me to lie down, and as soon as my head touches her lap, she runs her fingers through my hair.

"Why are you so cute?" she asks.

Cute? That's a new one.

She kisses my forehead. I look up to see her eyes shimmering in the moonlight. "No matter what happens, just know that I'm sincere."

HELLO FEELINGS
Thursday

Last night was everything I could've imagined. Riley and I stayed up all night. We talked until 1 A.M. I learned more about her and her family, they're from Columbia. She mentioned how close she is to her brother Miguel. He's two years older and lives in Los Angeles. Get this, he's also a mechanic. I also found out that she's close with her mother but not with her father. I told her more about me including the story of how Leah and I met. It was really important to me for her to know why we spend so much time together. I regaled her with the story of the day I scraped my leg at the park and how Leah came to the rescue.

I had set my phone alarm for 9 A.M. to get a head start to Jessie's. On my way there, I try calling Reece several times so he can meet me there, but no response. After about fifteen minutes, I get a text from him asking to meet up first at his place, along with an address. My phone starts ringing, and without seeing who it is, I answer. Screaming is the only thing I hear on the line.

"Leah? What's wrong?" The phone is connected to my car speakers, so I have to lower the volume.

"I just checked your location, and you've been nowhere near home."

Of course, she's checking up on where I am; leave it up to her to play detective.

"And since I knew you were off today, that probably means you had a 'nightcap' last night."

I laugh and simply respond, "Nothing out of the ordinary happened, Leah. We stayed up just talking."

The line goes quiet for a moment. "Eww, why?"

I laugh again. Yesterday, she was ready to attack; now she wants Riley's and my relationship to progress. Typical Leah.

"I'm on my way to Reece's place."

If this traffic ever gets moving. It's a Thursday morning; shouldn't everyone be at work by now?

"Whoa, you're on your way to Ireland boy's house; I don't approve."

I didn't ask for her approval, but I'm ready for the lecture.

"This guy already has the hots for you, and now you're going to his place without backup?"

Reece doesn't come off to me as dangerous; he's very kind and considerate. Also, he doesn't like me in that way, so why does she keep saying it?

"Leah, we have been over this already; Reece is a good guy."

She smacks her lips.

"You returned home with a scar on your hand, had a panic attack, and passed out all on the same day because of him."

Why did I bother telling her all that? I should've known better.

After about twenty minutes of back and forth, I finally manage to make it to his house. Leah aggressively Facetimes me so I can show her my surroundings for some peace of mind.

"Are you happy now?" I ask.

I hold my phone with the camera facing the entrance to Reece's home.

"Can I hang up now?"

She shakes her head and insists she's staying on for a little while. I ring the doorbell.

"Look, he's coming at any moment now; this is ridiculous."

I hear the door being unlocked, and Reece appears with no shirt on, just a towel wrapped around his waist. There's a muscle on every part of his body. Is that an eight-pack? His voice breaks me out of my train of thought.

"Are you coming in?"

Still shocked at his appearance, I don't respond.

"Yes, he is," Leah responds.

"Hi, Leah. How are you?" Reece asks.

"I'm great, now remove that—" I disconnect the call.

This guy has a fantastic body. *Okay, Cameron focus, this is normal, right?* Guys see each other without clothes all the time. He knew you were coming, so he was just in the middle of getting dressed.

"Are you going to come inside or just stand out here?" His voice startles me back into the present.

I nod my head, and he moves aside as I step in. His house has a modern and contemporary feel to it.

Looking around, I notice the pendant light hanging from the ceiling and the plush, blue velvet sofa with matching chairs. It all goes nicely with the ombre-colored rug on top of the wooden floors.

"Did you decorate the place yourself?"

He walks towards me; he's standing close, and I can smell a sweet scent all over him.

He gives me a grin and places a hand on my shoulder. His gaze is quite intimidating.

"I did."

I swallow uncomfortably and gently move his hand away and walk towards the sofa.

"Where did you get your furniture?"

I rub the couch, feeling the softness against my skin. This must have cost a fortune. There's no way I could afford this on my salary.

His voice breaks through the silence. "It was shipped from London." Moving towards what must be his bedroom, he says, "Just give me a moment to get dressed."

I decide to look around while I wait. He has a large selection of music. There's a lot of country, pop, and some rock. I notice some pictures on the shelf; he seems close to his family. Who is that? Little Reece? Haha, he has on some overalls with a baseball cap. As I peruse the small gallery of images, one stands out to me the most. I pick it up to get a closer look. It's Reece and a beautiful brunette. She looks like a model, and I wouldn't be surprised if she was one with that body. In the bottom right-hand corner, I notice a handwritten message that says, "XOXO, love you forever". They are on a beach; she's wearing a coral-colored bikini while he's in coral and white swimming trunks. In the photo, he's lying on a towel on his stomach and she's draped across his back with a huge smile.

"That's Samantha." Startled by his voice, I drop the photo, Luckily the frame is sturdy.

"She and I were high school sweethearts."

He picks up the image and seems to gaze at it longingly. Is that a tear? Could she have been the one who got away? He seems a little tense now; maybe I should steer the conversation somewhere lighter.

"A good-looking guy like you probably had many sweethearts." I laugh and give him a shoulder tap.

Reece looks at me with those piercing grey eyes. I'm not sure why, but I feel so at ease when he looks at me. He steps closer and places his right hand on my shoulder. My heart instantly starts beating faster. He moves closer towards me until our noses are inches away.

"You think I'm good looking?"

I remove his hand from my shoulder and take a step back. "You're an attractive guy; anyone can see that."

He smirks and walks towards the kitchen. "Would you like something to drink, Cam?" He opens the fridge and starts naming different beverages. My options are water, juice, soda, and milk.

"I could use a bottle of water."

He surprises me by tossing the bottle my way and I surprise myself by catching it.

"I think we should head out now," he announces.

I nod my head and follow him outside. He has a grey Chevrolet Silverado and a grey Camaro. I wonder if he buys his cars to match his eyes. There was a time when I wanted a Camaro, but the cost seemed a bit too much. My blue Jeep Compass has been working just fine for me.

"I thought maybe we could drive my truck."

I agree and follow him. I knew these trucks were huge, but didn't realize how huge. Luckily, I pull myself up on the first attempt. The grey and black leather seats inside feel warm. It's hot out, but he had both vehicles parked under his shed. Before I can complement his truck, he shifts towards me. I can feel his breath against my skin; and his grey eyes looking right through me. What is happening? *Please don't kiss me, please don't kiss me…* He places his hand behind me on the headrest.

"Just thought I'd help with your seatbelt." He makes even that piece of information sound seductive.

Okay, Cameron, pull yourself together; he's not making a move on you. Still, he's too close.

I'm starting to get a little flustered here.

"I can do it; just put yours on," I reply nervously.

I try pulling, but it won't budge. After several awkward attempts, I'm able to secure my seatbelt. I glance over to see him smiling.

"Ready."

HELLO NURSERY

Upon our approach to their house, I see Jessie and Amber sitting on the porch. He is rubbing her belly while she rests her head on his shoulders. Judging by her facial expression, he must've just said something funny. At work, Jessie's known for his sense of humor and the love he has for his family. He looks up as we pull in the driveway and waves with a massive grin on his face. Once the truck is parked, a sizeable German shepherd comes running. I immediately start to panic. I do like dogs, but I may be a little terrified of them. Reece notices my behavior and strolls over and starts petting him. What's with this guy? For all he knows that dog could've instantly attacked.

"You're full of surprises," he says to me.

What does he mean by "surprises"? There are a lot of people in the world who are afraid of dogs.

"Are you guys ready?" Jessie asks.

I am too focused on the dog to respond.

"He's friendly, Cameron."

Yeah, that's what most owners say. Before you know it, they jump on you and start barking.

And between the sharp teeth and claws, they can instantly do damage even if it's not intentional.

"Come here boy." Jessie kneels, and the dog immediately jumps on him, wagging his tail.

"Good boy, Max." He begins licking Jessie's face.

He does seem friendly, but I don't want to take any chances just yet.

"I'll wait in here."

Jessie looks up at me and laughs, but picks up Max and heads inside while Amber follows. Eventually we do too and Jessie gives us a tour. The house has two bedrooms, a fireplace, and a laundry room, which looks large enough to be turned into a bedroom, too. Then, he takes us into the nursery located next to the master bedroom. There are several baby items still in boxes on the floor.

"Sorry about the mess; we haven't had much time to organize everything," Jessie says, sliding some of the boxes towards one side of the room.

Between his work schedule and doctor visits with Amber, I can understand the limited amount of time he has.

"So, Reece, how long have you known Cameron?" Jessie asks, continuing to move more boxes.

"Not long, but it feels like much more."

He looks over at me and smiles. I return his expression awkwardly.

"He's a good guy."

He must be in a great mood. Two compliments back-to-back.

"Any update on the due date?" I ask, hoping to avoid any further questioning from Jessie; it's not because I'm uncomfortable, but I don't want Reece to feel that way.

"Any day now."

He continues to tell us how the most recent visit was just a check-up and how the doctor informed him to stand by.

"Jessie, come here," Amber yells from somewhere nearby.

He runs out of the room. Reece and I stare at each other for a moment. I'm still unable to get image of him half-dressed from earlier today out of my mind. I don't think it was inappropriate; I'm just taken back by how he was so comfortable around me, not fully clothed. He nudges my shoulder.

"What's wrong?" he asks.

I start pulling pieces to the crib out of a box. It looks like there are letters on each one.

Now, where are the instructions? I start digging deeper.

"Cameron?"

With the noise I'm making while rooting around the pieces, I assumed he would forget about his question and start helping. Instead, he kneels and grabs my hand. My heart instantly starts racing. I look up to see his mesmerizing grey eyes looking back at mine. Unable to speak or move, I just maintain my gaze. I can't help but wonder what is going through his mind.

"What is it, Cameron?"

I pull my hand back out of the box with the instruction manual. "I found it." I laugh nervously. Then I unfold the instructions and start reading them, but Reece snatches them out of my grasp.

He grabs my arm and pulls me closer towards him. He stares right into my eyes.

"Did I do something wrong?" he asks softly.

He releases my arm after realizing how uncomfortable I am.

"No, I'm just anxious to see how the crib turns out."

He exhales loudly and turns away from me. He seems really troubled. Think, Cameron; what could you do to ease his mind?

"What are we doing after this?" It was the first thing I could think of to change the conversation.

He looks up at me. "Let's go out tonight."

Go out? On a Thursday? Where could we possibly go today? No way, please don't say… "How about this lounge kind of place with dancing?" he asks.

I could give multiple reasons why I don't want to go, but I don't want him to question me any further about something being wrong.

"Okay," I say and double down with a nod. "What club?"

A sly grin appears on his face. What could he be thinking?

"How about Vibrations?"

I'm not familiar with the place. Well, I'm not aware of many places since I don't really drink or do nights out. I guess it sounds like it could be fun. "Let's do it."

He laughs at my response and hands me back the instructions.

HELLO ANSWERS

It takes us two hours to get the nursery together; Jessie was unable to help while tending to Amber, but checked in on us a few times. He thanked us and offered to feed us, but we decided to head out so we could get dressed for whatever place Reece was taking me to. The ride back is more relaxed. We sing along to the radio and laugh about childhood memories. Reece mentions that while tagging along with his older cousins he once went up to the top of an abandoned building and ran around on the roof, perilously close to the edge. He said he remembers being more exhilarated than scared. It's probably why he loves rock climbing so much. He injured his back once, but said it was one of the happiest moments of his life. He says he wanted to try and fly. I told him that when I climbed a fence once and my shorts got stuck, causing me to hang upside, I cried like a baby. By the time I was able to get down, I had scratches all over my legs.

Once we pull up to my complex, I immediately notice Leah's blue Camry parked in the lot. I wonder how long she's been here.

"I'll be back in an hour," Reece says to me as I get out of his truck.

Once I get to my front door, I can hear Leah's muffled voice on the other side. It sounds like she's yelling. I place my ear to the door, hoping to hear more clearly. I can't make out much of anything she's saying. I open the door, and she looks up surprised and quickly disconnects the call.

"Who was that?" I ask.

"Anthony!" Based on her tone, she wasn't too happy with the conversation before I walked in.

"So, how'd the nursery help go?" she asks.

That look alone lets me know she wants to hear all about Reece. The video call where she saw him in a towel may have prompted several questions for her.

"After a lot of trial and error, we finished," I reply.

I walk to my bedroom, where she follows and watches me as I look for something to wear. I probably should've asked Reece more about the place tonight. I'm sure something casual should work.

"What happened at his place?" she demands.

I turn around to see her standing so close I can smell the marinara sauce on her breath. She backs me into a wall, waiting for a response.

"Nothing happened." I move around her and continue searching through my clothes. Maybe I should wear a polo shirt and shorts, at least I'd be comfortable. She grabs my arm, pulling me to face her.

"You're lying." She folds her arms, waiting for another answer.

"I'm serious." I walk over to my closet and find a blue and white floral print polo shirt. I think I have some white shorts in here somewhere as well.

"Oh my… did he make a move on you?"

Okay, now she's getting a little too excited about this. "He didn't do anything, Leah." I brush past her and go over to the dresser.

"He only had on a towel. Did you at least…" I slam the drawer and look at her.

"What's going on with you and Anthony?"

Looking defeated, she plops down on the edge of my bed and lies back with a loud sigh. I follow her lead and do the same. We both stare up at the ceiling.

"I still haven't told him."

Feeling powerless, I just stay still, what advice do I give? I know from the talk I had with Anthony, he loves her, and with everything that's happening with her, she still loves him. Why is it so hard to tell someone how you feel? We give ourselves pep talks about how everything will be okay, yet we're afraid of being vulnerable and honest with our feelings.

"I'm scared, Cam."

I reach over and pull her into a hug. I can't remember the last time we were lying in the bed like this, sharing our feelings.

"He's a great guy," I tell her. Part of me wants to let her know I've talked to him, but another part of me fears how she might respond after I promised not to get involved. "And you're a smart woman." This is the time for me to be supportive and encourage her to do the right thing.

"You'll find the words to say." She hugs me tighter. "If it doesn't go as planned; I'll be here."

We made a promise to be there for each other years ago. I've kept that promise ever since. I was there for a lot of her first experiences, just as she was for mine. I would do all I can to protect her, and she'd do the same for me. She looks up and kisses my chin.

"I love you, Cam."

I kiss her forehead. "I love you too, Leah."

After a few more moments of lying there, I get up and continue looking for some shorts to wear.

"Where are you going?!" she asks a little too loudly.

"Out!"

She folds her arms and follows me back to the closet.

"With whom?"

Instead of answering, I continue digging through clothes.

"Riley?"

Aha! I find the shorts. But Leah snatches them, staring at me and waiting for a response.

"Reece!" I say, grabbing the shorts back.

"Where to?"

I walk towards the bathroom and wet a washcloth. I worked up a sweat working on the crib and need to clean off my face.

"He's taking me to some lounge."

"A lounge? Which one?" she demands.

"Vibrations!" I answer, still wiping my face. After a few seconds of silence, I turn towards her. She stands there smiling silently.

"What?" I ask.

She grabs me and starts jumping and screaming. Still confused at her response, I just stand there.

"Cam, have you never heard of Vibrations?" I shake my head no.

"Oh, Cam… it's a gay club!"

HELLO WILD SIDE

Once we get to Vibrations, I notice neon-colored lights on the wall. It looks sort of fancy from the outside, so I'm glad I wore the nice jeans that Leah suggested. Reece has on black denim, a grey crewneck shirt, and a jacket. The bouncer checks our IDs.

"Try not to get too wasted," he says in a very unexcited monotone.

He pulls the rope aside for us, and we enter. The interior has industrial walls, smooth flooring, and more lights.

"How many?" a woman at a podium asks while pointing at the glow sticks.

I look over to Reece, who holds up two fingers. She hands them over to him. He then takes a step closer to me and attaches one of the glow sticks around my neck. His sandalwood vanilla scent from earlier is still lingering. He hands me a glow stick with another string.

"Do you mind putting on mine?" he asks.

I begin creating a knot around the glow stick loop. I struggle a bit due to sweaty fingers. It also doesn't help that he's staring at me. Not once does he look to make sure I'm tying it correctly; instead, he just stares me right in the eyes. He moves closer towards me and I try to secure the glow stick around his neck as quickly as possible. Once completed, he doesn't lean back. Instead, he continues staring.

We continue walking down the hall with the neon lights, which start changing colors the further we go. There are a lot of people dancing; the space here is enormous and the electronic music is pretty good.

Hanging from the ceiling is a metal grid hung with lights. It seems to be the main source of illumination for the club; areas further away seem pretty dark. The spiral staircase in the center of the dance floor has small bulbs fitted into each tread. It leads to another floor with minimal lighting.

"Thoughts?"

I jump, startled by his breath on my ear. He stands next to me, waiting on a response.

"I like it."

He grabs my wrist and pulls me forward, parting the crowd.

"Excuse me, excuse me," I keep saying until I bump into a couple kissing. It's two beautiful women; one with pink hair and the other with purple.

"I'm sorry."

They sneer at me and continue kissing. I look at Reece, and we continue walking through all the dancers until we reach a bar.

"Is this your first time here?" he asks and I nod yes.

A male bartender appears in front of us with no shirt; just suspenders and pants. He has a very chiseled body. This is the part I dread, drinking alcohol. "What can I get you, fellas?"

"One margarita and one mojito," Reece responds.

Whoa, two real drinks already. Maybe I should start with water.

"The margarita is yours."

What? Why would he order for me?

"It's a tequila cocktail."

I look towards the left side of the bar to see a guy with longish, orange hair and a sharp nose staring at me. He has on a skintight, long sleeve shirt. He raises his glass to me. To my right is a woman with a fade haircut talking on her cell phone. She looks annoyed.

The bartender appears with our drinks. The taller glass has a lime hanging on the rim with what looks like sugar. The other has a lot of mint leaves and what appears to be a lime inside.

Reece slides the shorter glass to me. He raises his drink and I do the same.

"To new beginnings!" he yells over the music.

We clink our glasses. Once the drink touches my lips, it instantly burns. This tastes terrible; what do they mix in here? Also, who thought of putting salt on the rim of a glass?

I'm not an alcohol expert, but I thought margaritas were supposed to taste sweet. I look over to Reece and realize he's finishing his drink in one gulp. He slams his glass on the counter and looks at mine.

"Come on, Cam." He lifts my glass to my lips and mouths, "Drink."

"What's in it?" I ask.

"Tequila, lime juice, and Cointreau." He gazes at me. "It's shaken, not stirred."

"What's in yours?" I continue the questioning.

He sits on the barstool and signals me to sit as well. "Mint leaves, white rum, lime juice, and simple syrup."

He knows his drinks.

"Are you going to finish it?" he asks.

I shake my head no. He takes my glass and empties it in one gulp as well.

"Do you like oranges?" he asks.

Of course I like oranges, what kind of question is that? I nod my head yes. He signals the bartender over.

"Can I get two screwdrivers?"

I've never heard of them, but I'm willing to try anything other than what I just had.

"I'm glad you came out with me," he says, his lips almost touching my ear.

As loud as the music is, that seems to be the better option instead of yelling.

"Thanks for inviting me."

The man with the orange mid-length hair stands right next to Reece and me.

"Hey guys."

I wave and Reece nods his head.

"Let's dance." A sly grin appears on the guy's face.

I'm not a dancer, so I guess I'll sit this one out.

"I'll wait for the drinks if you want to dance," I say to Reece.

He looks between the guy and me. "I'll stay here with you."

The guy sits in the chair next to me smiling. He has on cut-up, light blue denim jeans. He runs his hand through his hair and leans towards me.

"I'm Alex."

He extends his hand. Reece steps forward and grabs it.

"I'm Reece."

He and Alex stare at each other for a moment before they release their grip.

"And you are?" he asks, looking over at me.

"I'm Cameron," I respond nervously.

His eyes are a bit glassy. You can also tell he's had some cocktails based on the alcohol on his breath, but he doesn't seem to be too drunk. A female bartender with suspenders arrives with our drinks. I hand Reece his, then grab mine. Like before, he finishes in one gulp. I take a sip of mines. The sweetness is there, but it's faint. Instead of complaining, I continue taking small sips. "Now that the introductions are out of the way, what do you say?" Alex says. I look over to Reece, who's glaring at Alex; he seems upset.

I don't want to be the cause of ruining the night. I lift the glass to my lips and start chugging. Although it burns, I finish it. After a few seconds, I let out a burp. I stand up, glancing between the two of them, both looking surprised at me at finishing the drink like that.

"Let's go," I announce.

I grab Reece's wrist, and Alex grabs mine as we head over to the dance floor. Once we reach the center, Alex removes his shirt and starts moving his hips to the music. I am a little taken aback by this. Then he signals for me to join him. I take a step back into Reece.

I look up to see his beautiful grey eyes staring at me while he's smiling. He looks over to Alex and removes his shirt and jacket. He places his shirt in his back pocket and hands me his jacket. They both start moving to the fast-paced music. I can't resist laughing; there's too much testosterone between these two. The woman who gave us our drinks at the bar appears, walking on the dance floor.

She has a tray full of small glasses, which I assume are shots. She stops in front of me.

"Would you like to try one?"

Overwhelmed, I stare at the tray full of glasses; each one is a different color.

"Which do you recommend?"

She hands me a pink one with candy at the bottom. I drink it in one gulp, which is a mistake. I instantly start coughing and she gives me a couple of pats on the back. The after-taste is decidedly cinnamon.

"That was a fireball," she says, smiling.

I hand her back the glass, and she proceeds to make an offering to Alex and Reece. They both chug down one shot and then grab another, barely stopping to dance; these guys can drink. Alex looks as if he could be a professional dancer. Both of them look over and pull me between them. Reece takes off my jacket and tosses it to the floor. Alex removes my shirt. Instead of resisting, I join in with the dancing. The lights in the grid started changing colors. I look over to Reece. I now know that I had made the right choice to come out with him tonight.

26

HELLO COURAGE

An hour has passed by, and we are still on the dance floor. Multiple bartenders have walked by handing out shots; I lost count of how many I've had. I've been so pumped jumping around to the music playing. The tension between Alex and Reece went away; it's nice to see them getting along.

"I'm heading to the restroom," Alex says and walks away.

The light from the overhead grid fixture turns blue; the music shifts to something softer. Reece and I stand there looking around the dance floor. A lot of couples start wrapping their arms around each other. There's one couple near the corner I can't help but focus on. After they finish kissing, one of the women places her head on the other's shoulder while they slowly turn around. As the other face comes into view, I let out a gasp. Is it…?! I make my way through the crowd trying to get closer for a better view. I have to make sure that it's her, but before I can get any closer, a tug on my arm spins me around.

Reece is looking at me with concern. "Are you okay?"

I turn my attention back to where I'd been looking, but she's gone. I continue pushing my way through the crowd, a few push back. Another tug on my arm stops me.

"Cam!' Reece grabs my face, and the look in his eyes lets me know he was starting to panic. I don't want to worry him, but I just had to make sure my eyes weren't playing tricks on me. That couldn't have been Riley; I must've been so lost in my thoughts. By the time I start to give Reece my full attention, his face is close to mine.

I place my hands on his shoulders, squeezing them to assure him that I'm okay. Instead of him pulling away, he just continues to gaze into my eyes. My heart is beating fast. I take a step back, but he keeps coming closer. What's wrong with him? He places his hand behind my neck to bring me closer. Now I'm inches from his face.

And then I burp.

Mortified by what's just happened, I cover my mouth and run towards the restroom, but there are a couple of men waiting in line. Pull yourself together, Cameron; stop freaking out. I start slapping my face, hoping it will knock some sense into me. I can't help but think about the couple I saw making out. Was it Riley? Maybe I should text her. I pull out my phone and begin typing. Once my message is ready to send, I pause and look at the time. It's 1:00 AM. What if it wasn't her? Even it was, it's a little weird to send her a message at this hour. Feeling defeated, I put my phone back into my pocket.

Just as the line of guys in front of me for the restroom finally moves up, I see Reece walking towards me. We stand in silence until more guys come out. Once we're inside, there are more neon-colored lights and each urinal is occupied, but there are two stalls available for use. I take the one furthest to the left. After latching the door, I wonder if Leah's night is going well. I know she'll be upset since I haven't kept her up to date about my night here. I hear a knock.

"It's occupied," I shoot back.

Another knock follows. I flush the toilet and open it to see Reece standing there.

"Are you not having fun?" he asks.

I wouldn't be out this late if I weren't.

"Tonight…has been awesome," I say with a grin.

Other than my body feeling heavy and a little sluggish, I'm having a great time. I give him a playful shove. He still doesn't have his shirt on. If you have this lovely body, why not keep it off, right? What does his workout consist of? Scanning his chest, shoulders and arms, I don't see any tattoos or piercings. Maybe he only has the one behind his ear. However, I haven't inspected his back. I spin him around to confirm my suspicion. Nope, nothing there either.

"See anything you like?" he asks.

He turns around, facing me again. I'm still grinning. He grabs my left ear, and I grab his.

"Thank you for coming into my life," he mumbles.

I release his ear and wrap him in a hug. Leah has been the only friend I've been close to like this. I feel comfortable with Reece, like I do with her. He's a fantastic guy I enjoy being around.

"Thank you for being you," I reply. He grabs my right ear. This time, he brings his face closer to mine. His lips are a few inches away—the scent of alcohol on his breath. I put up my arms between us to prevent him from getting any closer. He steps back. I start feeling nauseous and place a hand on my stomach and, with the other, brace myself against the wall to stop from falling. My hand slips, so I start to go down. Instantly, Reece grabs my shoulders and starts to lift me up.

Before I can say thank you, vomit pours out.

HELLO PANIC
Friday

The sound of cabinet doors opening and closing wakes me up. My head is pounding, and I feel nauseous.

"Ugh, Leah!" Why did she have to let herself into my place of all mornings.

I turn onto my left shoulder while pulling a pillow up to my face. I thought that would drown out the noise, but it doesn't work. I throw the pillow onto the floor. Once I open my eyes towards the sun beaming through the window, my eyes hurt from the light, and my head aches even worse. I turn on my back, looking up towards the ceiling. As I lie there, I wonder what time I got in. The last thing I remember was being on the dance floor. Also, seeing Riley, or at least what looked like Riley.

I turn to grab my phone on the nightstand to call Reece. As I'm reaching, I notice my phone is missing. And so are all of my clothes; the only thing I have on is underwear. I look around and realize that I'm not in my room. I jump out of bed, looking around for my pants. They aren't on the dresser or the chair near the corner. My shoes are also missing. *Okay, think, Cameron, what happened?* You were dancing with Reece and another guy. There were shots, lots of selfies, and then what…? Ugh, this is not good.

Why can't I remember? Okay, try not to panic; just find your phone and call Reece. I keep reminding myself that this is not a big deal. There are plenty of people who go out and drink.

Sometimes things can get murky. Who am I kidding? This is not okay. I'm undressed and in a place I'm not familiar with. Wait—I'm not alone. I hear someone from the other side of the door. I continue scanning the room, hoping to spot my phone or some clothing to cover up with. At any moment, whoever's out there could come in and see me half-naked. Inside a drawer, I find a pair of shorts and a shirt. Maybe I can sneak out the window. I walk over and open the blinds to see how far up I am. It appears that I'm on the second floor looking onto a backyard with trees and a fence. There's no way I can jump down without hurting myself. I close the blinds and place the shorts and shirt I found back inside the dresser. They don't belong to me, and I don't want their owner to come looking for me. The time on the clock display is 11:00 AM. Okay, you can figure a way out of this. Let's just walk outside the room and confront whoever.

I open the door and stick my head out to see if I can see anyone. There is only a small table in the hallway and I see that my cell phone and keys are sitting on it. I run to grab both items and notice my shoes are located underneath the table. Where are my clothes? I don't have much time to look for them. Instead, I unlock my phone to find that it is fully charged. I dial Leah's number, but there's no answer. I hear footsteps approaching and run back into the room. I place my ear to the door and listen. The footsteps have stopped.

I run over to the bed and begin calling Leah again, but still no answer. The doorknob starts to turn, and my heart races. Once it opens, I jump up! Oh. Once his face appears from behind the door, I instantly relax.

"Reece!"

He's standing in the doorway wearing grey shorts and a grey tank top. He looks me up and down.

I grab the pillow I threw down earlier to cover up. "Where am I?"

He steps fully into the room and shuts the door behind him. "Good morning to you, too."

He walks over to the chair, and sits watching me. Silence fills the room as I wait for him to say something.

"You're in my room."

I begin to feel at ease knowing where I am. Now I need the answer to the obvious question: where are my clothes? But instead of asking that, I first want to learn something else.

"What happened last night?"

He lifts himself up from the chair.

"You don't remember?"

Panic starts to rise in my chest. Why is he smiling? Nothing out of the ordinary could've happened, right? I step backwards, and he moves closer. What is with this guy? I continue backing up until I reach the bed.

"You passed out."

Yeah, but what happened after that?

"I carried you."

Wait! You did what? Who asked you to do that? I could've walked on my own, I'm sure of it.

"I brought you to my place." A sly smile appears on his face. "Your clothes were ruined." That explains me waking up in underwear.

"I undressed you."

Oh no, that's so embarrassing. He keeps inching his way closer to me as he speaks.

"Then we…"

No, no, no, there's no way he and I could have… This can't be happening right now; I would not do anything like that, even while drunk, or would I?

"…went to sleep."

I exhale. I am so relieved. I never imagine sleeping with another man. Crossing that line is something I don't feel I would ever get over. That could've ruined our friendship. I value Reece as a friend; I wouldn't want to jeopardize that over a drunken night.

"That is used for resting your head."

He snatches the pillow I was using to cover up. I quickly replace it with my hands.

"What happened to my clothes?" I ask.

"You vomited… Laundry should be finished soon."

"So…sorry"

I squeeze my way out of the tight spot between him and the bed and wrap myself with the blanket. He watches me as I do so. He walks over towards the dresser, pulls out a navy-blue crewneck tee and grey lounging pants, and hands them to me.

"Thank you," I respond and stand there waiting for him to leave.

He stares at me a little longer. "I believe we're past the point of shyness."

I place the blanket onto the bed and begin getting dressed as quickly as possible. He walks over to the door and turns around. "Breakfast is ready."

After Reece drops me off back home, I call Leah. The phone rings several times before it goes to voicemail. It's unlike her to avoid me. Usually she would have texted me by now. I receive a notification on my phone, but it's not from her; it's from Anthony asking if we could meet up. Our last conversation didn't go as planned. I'm sure he has more questions regarding the break-up. I respond by asking "when and where?" He texts, "5 pm." In two hours, I'm supposed to meet Riley for frozen yogurt, which shouldn't take long. Two hours after that, Reece and I are getting together for Laser Tag. I agree to meet Anthony; I can only avoid him for so long.

Before I put my phone down, it rings; it's Leah.

"Hello?"

"Tell me everything," she demands.

Though insistent, she sounds like she's in a good mood, but I wonder why she didn't answer any of my calls.

"I've tried getting ahold of you multiple times today; where have you been?"

She sighs heavily into the phone. "I was with my mom at the doctor's." The silence on the phone lets me know that it didn't go well. "There's not much improvement."

I wish I could hug her right now. "Where are you?"

"Cleaning up the kitchen."

I hear water running in the background. "I can be there in twenty minutes," I say.

"No need. After this, I have to run some errands." The sound of dishes clinking comes through the phone. "Now, how was your night?"

I explain in detail about as much as I can remember. She finds humor in my drunken night.

"I can't believe you threw up on him."

"Little Cam is all grown up?" is all I can offer. "I'm meeting Riley later today."

She sighs at the mention of her name.

"Leah, come on…" If Riley and I start dating, these two women must get along; I can't have my best friend and, hopefully, future girlfriend fighting all the time. "Can you at least try to like her?" After a few seconds, I can hear heavy breathing, which I take as a sign of Leah agreeing to give her another chance.

"Fine, but only because I love you."

"Thank you, Leah." We talk on the phone for about an hour before I have to get dressed and meet Riley.

HELLO TRUTH

On the drive to the yogurt shop, I am so anxious to meet Riley; it could be due to us possibly discussing the status of our relationship, but it's also about what I might have seen last night. I'm not entirely certain how I should approach the situation. I don't want to come off as too evasive or judgmental. I guess the worst thing that could happen would be her getting upset about an assumption of her sexuality. Once I'm there, I see Riley standing near the entrance in blue jeans and a yellow tank top. Due to the nearly full lot, I have to find somewhere to park near the back. On my way walking towards the shop, I get a text from Recce. It's a picture taken of me biting an omelet he made earlier for breakfast. I can't help but laugh and respond with a thumbs up. Once I make it to the entrance, Riley embraces me tightly. I inhale the familiar fragrance and return her hug.

"What flavor are you having today?" she asks.

Although there's my usual go-to, I figure I'll switch it up. I release the hug and look at her.

"Any suggestions?"

She grabs my arm to walk us inside. Today of all days the place seems busier than expected; we look around for a bit to see if there's anywhere to sit. I notice a place near the back wall and point it out.

"You grab the free spot and I'll get the yogurt," she says.

I nod my head in agreement and begin making my way towards the table. As I sit down, I receive an alert from my phone; another text from Reece. "Hope you're ready for Laser Tag tonight. Don't forget to wear something relaxed." I wasn't sure if I would have enough time to go back and change clothes after I meet with Anthony, so I wore olive pants with a black crewneck t-shirt. I begin typing. "Shouldn't you be the one worried about being prepared?" And how relaxed do you have to be for Laser Tag? I remember going once with Leah and a few friends; some were casually dressed, while others wore activewear. A heavily dressed-up bowl of frozen yogurt interrupts my thoughts. Riley has combined chocolate syrup, chocolate drops, chocolate shavings, caramel syrup, and whipped cream. I look over at her bowl; gummy bears, gummy worms, and Skittles.

"What flavor is this?" I ask, pointing at the dish in front of me.

She grins and tilts her head to the side.

"Try it." She pushes the bowl closer and then hands me a spoon. The presentation is not appetizing and is a mouthful of cavities waiting to happen. I lift out a spoonful of the concoction, and there is a lot of chocolate dripping over. I place it inside my mouth. Hmm, bittersweet, but to my surprise, it's not as bad as I thought it would be. Although not terrible, it's just not something I would consider ordering in the future.

"Salted caramel," she announces.

That's actually one of the flavors I always pass up visiting any yogurt shop. As if reading my mind, she grabs my bowl and switches it with hers.

"I have this every time I come." She dips her spoon in and eats a mouthful.

"Since you had mango last time, I got you strawberry."

I didn't expect her to remember, but it's nice to know she pays attention.

"Thank you," I respond.

I lift a spoonful of the yogurt and toppings from the new bowl, and it is tasty—the sweet and savory taste of strawberry. After we finish our yogurt, we decide to sit outside. Now is the chance for me to ask about us.

"So Riley, I've been thinking, and I wanted—"

She places a hand over my mouth. Staring into my eyes, she places a hand behind my neck. She pulls me closer into a kiss. This kiss is much different from the last one. This time it's soft and tender. At this moment, I feel wanted. She wraps her arms around my neck, and we continue kissing passionately.

"Riley!" A voice screams out from behind me. It's Mercedes standing there with a look of utter disbelief. She runs over and physically separates Riley and me. "What's going on?!" she demands.

Riley stands there fearfully. What does she have to be afraid of?

"I'm waiting."

Riley begins rubbing her arms and tearing up. "I'm sorry," she says, looking over at me.

I'm confused, but I step closer and begin wiping her tears. Mercedes grabs my arm and pushes me away. What is her problem? Riley steps in between us and faces Mercedes.

"Please don't be upset."

"You promised me!" Mercedes yells.

What is going on?

"I know it's just…"

"Does he know?" Mercedes says, pointing at me.

I know that *you're* overreacting.

"We said we were going to work on it," she continues.

Riley turns towards me and moves closer. Tears are streaming down both cheeks when she grabs both of my hands.

"Cam… Mercedes is my girlfriend."

I'm aware of that; she mentioned it the night at the club.

"Yeah, but it's not right for her to overreact," I respond, looking at Mercedes.

She gives me a mean stare. Riley grabs both of my hands then looks up into my eyes.

"Cameron, she's not *that* kind of girlfriend."

Still unsure of what she's trying to say, I walk closer to Mercedes.

"This is no way to treat a friend." Riley grabs my arm and pulls me closer back to her. "She's my partner, Cameron." I freeze.

"We're a couple, but…"

I shake my hands free of her. These last few days of me wanting to get to know her, to spend time with her was because I wanted to be with her. I knew we couldn't call ourselves a couple yet, but I didn't expect the bigger reason we couldn't be was because she was already in a relationship…with another woman.

"I was afraid I wasn't clear enough when I mentioned it to you the first time," Riley says.

Yeah, you're weren't clear. Leah was right; I wasted too much time thinking that a girl as confident and beautiful as her would be interested in me.

"I planned on clearing things up, but—"

I raise my hands, signaling for her to stop. I don't want to hear any more lies from her. I was thinking I could build a future with her all this time.

"Our relationship is complicated," Mercedes chimes in.

My phone rings, and I pull it out to see Anthony's name appear on the screen. Instead of answering, I put it back into my pocket. "I have to go," I respond and begin to turn around.

Riley pulls onto my arm. "Can I at least finish explaining?"

I turn towards her and remove her hands. "Take care, Riley." I try to say this with little emotion, but a tear rolls down my cheek.

I sprint through the parking lot, trying to get out of here as quickly as possible. My eyes begin to sting due to the flood of tears now welling up. Once I get to my car, I start kicking the door. *I can't believe this; I finally decided to let someone in again, and this happens.* I get inside and begin pounding on the steering wheel.

HELLO HEARTBREAK

Anthony and I decided to meet at his place since my time with Riley ended sooner than expected. His home is about twenty minutes away from the yogurt shop. Once I arrive, I decide to sit in the car a little longer to pull myself together. I don't want my emotions to affect the conversation about him and Leah. I walk up to the second floor of his apartment complex and knock on the door a couple of times before he answers. He's wearing his work-out clothes.

"I was in the middle of exercising when you called." He heads into the kitchen, but I take a seat on the couch, waiting for him to return.

"Would you like something to drink?" he yells.

"No, thanks."

After a few minutes, he comes back with a bottle of blue-colored water. It must be his post-work-out drink.

"Okay, now what's going on with Leah?" he asks.

I get up and begin pacing back and forth, trying to figure out the words to explain things. In a situation like this, there's not much you can say without being yelled at after.

"Have you had a chance to talk with Leah lately?" I ask.

He slumps back on the couch, looking up at the ceiling. "Barely. She doesn't stay on the phone long enough to really call it talking. Cameron, I need to know what is happening with her."

Should I tell him or not? Maybe I could give him just enough information, so he won't think he did anything wrong.

"Leah is under a lot of stress right now." It's not a lie. Being pregnant and confused would be very stressful, right? With pregnancy comes many different emotions, and sometimes those emotions can be confusing, which could make someone possibly overthink things.

"Stress about what?" he asks, interrupting my thoughts.

"Her future," I respond.

Okay, maybe I didn't think this all the way through. I should just leave and tell him to call Leah. But that might only make the situation worst. Not just for him, but for me too. It's bad enough I'm sneaking behind my best friend's back, involving myself in something she clearly said not to.

Although my intentions are only to help her, she might not see it that way. My phone begins to ring. It's Leah... Why did she have to pick this exact moment to call? I can't pick up; Anthony will know it's her, and she'll know I'm here.

"That's not answering the question, Cameron." He stands up, raising his voice. Anthony then walks in front of me, preventing me from any further pacing. "Look, I understand you care for her, but I'm *her man*." He's speaking calmly. "You have to know that I love her and will do whatever I can to make her happy." He grabs my shoulders and stares into my eyes.

I've thought many times about how Anthony may feel, but I never really realized how painful this has been for him until now and seeing him like this. However, I'm hurting from what happened between Riley and me, it's nowhere near what he's most likely feeling. I remove his hands and sit on the couch. I pat a spot next to me. He plops down and looks back up at the ceiling.

"I know you love her, and she knows that, too," I assure him. Okay, Cameron, it's now or never. "Anthony, Leah's—"

A pounding on the door interrupts us. Anthony runs to look out the peephole. Was he expecting someone? Once he opens the door, he's shoved out of the way. I wasn't expecting her to be here. At least not now, not when we'd almost cleared things up.

"What is this?" Leah demands.

I stand up, not knowing what to say or do.

"Leah…" is all Anthony manages to say before she glares at him.

"I'm talking to Cam." She looks back at me with the same glare in her eyes. She throws her bag at me, waiting for a response. "Well!" she raises her voice once again.

I've never seen her this upset with me before.

"I came to talk with Anthony," I respond.

She approaches me with clenched fists and a tight jaw. "About what?" she asks.

I take a few steps back. I've seen a few people who've been on the opposite side of her frustration.

"I wanted to clear some things up," I say.

She shakes her head in disbelief. She begins pacing, running one hand through her hair while the other is on her hip. "I specifically asked you not to get involved." She removes her jacket and throws it at me. "I told you when I was ready, I would handle it." Tears begin to form in her eyes.

I attempt to hug her, but she pushes me away.

"Leah, I didn't—" I start to say, but before I can finish my sentence, she looks up at me with a paralyzing glare.

"Shut up Cameron!" she yells. "I asked you not to get involved."

I hold my head down, unsure of what to say next. I know she's upset that I've gone behind her back, but I haven't mentioned her pregnancy.

"Leah, if you—"

She smacks me across my face. I'm stunned. I know there is nothing else I can say that would change this moment. I place my hand where the pain is starting to tingle.

My eyes begin to burn with tears.

"Get out!" she shouts.

I don't want to leave with things like this, but I know there will be no getting through to her when she's this mad. Once I make it in the doorway, I stop. "I didn't tell him, but maybe now, you will." I slam the door behind me.

I run to the stairwell and can't help but cry. First Riley, now Leah. Today is not going as I expected it would. The worst part about this is my betrayal of my best friend. I never wanted to cause her any pain; I only wanted to help release as much anxiety as I could. Between work, doctor visits with her mom, her break up with Anthony, and this pregnancy, I only thought I could talk to Anthony and calm him down. Maybe if he knew he did nothing wrong, he would stop bothering Leah about what he thought he might've done. My phone begins to ring, and without looking, I answer.

"Hello." I start wiping my eyes and sniffling. Reece's voice comes through the phone.

"Cameron, what's wrong?"

I begin crying even harder, unsure of what to say or where to start.

"Do you need me to come over?"

I run down the stairs, making my way towards my car. I'm so overwhelmed, I can barely use my keys to open the door and get in.

"Yes..."

HELLO COMFORT

It takes me about thirty minutes to make it back to my place; Reece is already waiting outside the door. I embrace him in a hug.

"What happened?" he asks with sincerity.

We stand in the hallway to my apartment hugging a bit longer before we just sit on the floor.

"Leah and I fought," I finally say. "But in a way that we never have."

He puts his hand over my shoulder and pulls me closer to him. "About what?"

I raise myself and look down the hallway. I was hoping Leah would call or even come over so we could make things right. It's scary to know that our friendship is at risk.

"We don't have to talk about it."

I look over at him and begin to cry again. He stands and pulls me up into a hug and starts rubbing my back.

"I brought something to cheer you up." He hands over a plastic bag filled with ice cream cartons and cookies. Excitement rushes through me as I begin unlocking the door.

"Let's go inside before it melts," I say.

We head into the kitchen and sit on the high chairs. I pour the contents of the bag onto the counter. There's vanilla ice cream, caramel ice cream, and rocky road, along with Oreos, chocolate chips cookies, and shortbread cookies. I grab two bowls and two spoons.

"Wouldn't it be better to eat from the pints?" he asks.

I collect the bowls and place them back in the cabinet.

"Agreed."

I remove the vanilla ice cream lid and open the Oreo cookies; we both dig in. After about ten minutes of silence, he grabs my hand.

"Look whatever happened, I want you to know I'm here for you." I squeeze his hand. I eat another spoon of ice cream.

"Leah and I fought due to a misunderstanding."

"Have you tried clearing it up?

"I didn't have the words to; it's a sensitive topic."

"Fair enough. Maybe you should just wait a day or two; it'll give you both some time to think."

"Also, I found out Riley is dating someone else."

He begins choking, and his face turns red, but manages to ask, "Are you okay?"

I nod my head yes. "Her girlfriend saw us kissing."

He begins choking again. I go over and begin patting his back. "Maybe we should stop eating cookies and ice cream." I walk over to the fridge and hand him a bottle of water.

"No, it's okay," Reece says. He opens the water and takes a gulp.

"I left before she could tell me how long they've been dating."

"How come?"

There are so many reasons I could give.

"I can't choose one emotion to describe how I was feeling." I grab the ice cream and a pack of cookies and head over to the couch in the living room. He follows and sits next to me.

"Maybe I'm meant to be alone."

A tear rolls down the right side of my cheek as I continue eating ice cream. I didn't expect to have so many feelings coming at once. Yes, I am indeed sad, but I'm also upset, confused, and curious. How long did Riley plan on keeping this from me? It now makes sense why Mercedes was so possessive of their relationship. Although I have mixed feelings, I hadn't even been thinking about how she might feel. Also, what am I going to do about the situation with Leah? Reece wipes away my tears as they begin to fall.

"No one's meant to be alone," he says softly.

I look up to see his eyes are starting to water too. I don't want my pain to affect him; maybe I should change the topic.

"How are things with you?" I ask, wiping my nose.

He gives me a little grin and leans back into the sofa.

"Well, I met someone."

This is awesome. I want to know more, but I don't want him to think I'm nosy. I turn sidewise to let him know he has my full attention.

"They're kind and thoughtful…"

Okay, great start, please continue. He looks over to me and smiles. I return his expression, and he turns his body towards me.

"Also, they're smart and beautiful."

It sounds like a match. *Okay, now give me a name.*

"But I don't think they're available right now."

What! That's it? Nothing else to go on, just a possibility in your mind?

"What makes you think that?" I ask.

He walks back into the kitchen and grabs the rocky road pint of ice cream and chocolate chip cookies. He pulls the lid off and places it on the coffee table and begins eating. I look down to see we were almost out of vanilla and Oreos.

"Just a feeling I have."

"Does this person have a name?" I ask anxiously.

Based on his laughter, I can only assume he knows how much I want to know.

"I'll tell you when the time is right."

I scoop the last bit of vanilla ice cream from the container. He watches me as I throw the carton away. I receive an alert from my phone and quickly pull it out, hoping it's Leah, but it's Riley. Do I want to read what this says? Maybe I should wait until I'm alone. I don't want to overwhelm myself with too many emotions in one day. I still have to try and make things right with Leah. I unlock my phone and begin to type a message to Leah but stop. When she wants to talk, I'm sure she'll reach out. Just like I need space from Riley, she may need space from me. Maybe I can text Anthony. I begin typing.

I look at the time and notice that Reece and I have been talking for over an hour. Also, it's thirty minutes until 7:00 PM. I spin around and run back to the Reece on the sofa.

"Are we still doing Laser Tag?" I ask.

He places the lid back onto the ice cream and says, "I think that would be a great way to take your mind off things for the moment."

I nod my head in agreement and begin putting on my shoes.

"I'll meet you at my truck," he says, walking out the door.

It felt chilly earlier, so I grab my coat, but before I can open the door, I get an alert. It's a text from Anthony. "Hey Cam, she's still here. We've talked about a few things but haven't discussed why she wants to take a break. She's still mad about you and me talking, but I'm hoping she'll stay the night instead of driving when she's upset. I'll keep you updated if anything changes."

I respond with an "ok." Some progress is being made. Better that she opens up slowly to him than not at all.

HELLO UNEXPECTED

The drive to Laser Tag takes about twenty minutes. It's in a tall, grey building full of people laughing and talking about how much fun they had. There are also several arcade machines to play.

"I'll get the tickets," Reece says, walking away to the attendant.

Although the place is bit loud for my taste, there's something joyful about seeing all these families and friends enjoying themselves. I notice a couple of couples holding hands near the gumball machine. It makes me think of what life could've been like with Riley. To my right is an elderly man and woman laughing about their scores from their game. That reminds me of the times Leah and I spent joking around with each other about test scores. When we both sat for the ACT in high school, we were determined to do better than the other. Whoever got the lowest would be the one to treat the other to lunch. Then there was a time when we were a little too competitive playing baseball. The loser had to let the winner cut their hair. Leah won and came over with clippers that afternoon. My mom and dad were so upset once they saw the crazy, uneven haircut. I wish I could call her and laugh about old memories. A tap on my shoulder interrupts my thoughts. I turn around to see the joy on Reece's face; he's holding up a ticket in each hand.

"Are you ready to be defeated?" he asks, handing over one to me.

I pull it from him and try to return the same enthusiasm in his voice.

"Are you?" I ask with unconvincing bravado.

He signals for me to follow. Our tickets get collected at the entrance of a dark hallway. We pass through heavy, black curtains to enter a minimally lit room where we can make out a lot of boulders spread out. From the looks of this place, one would think it's a maze.

"Alright, guys and gals, the vests are located here to your left," the instructor announces.

"Could you please put them on?"

There are a few sets of vests with lights embedded in them. Half are blue and the other half are red. There are a total of eight people inside putting on the vests, including us.

Reece grabs a red one while I take a blue one. After securing our vests, the instructor hands us our weapons. Each is color-coded to our vests.

"I would like four people to a team. Please, no shoving or touching during the game."

After ten minutes of explaining the rules, he leads us into the field.

"Once the music stops, the game is over."

The countdown begins, and everyone spreads out. I decide to run into one of the tunnels nearby. I figure this would be a great spot to hide out in. After the countdown horn sounds off, the lights became even dimmer, making it difficult to see. I continue walking further into the tunnel, seeing where it leads. Once I make it to the other side, I see steps that lead up to another level. I follow them to the top and discover a guy with a red-lighted vest. I hide behind the nearest boulder I can find.

After a few seconds, I aim at his vest and pull the trigger. His light starts flashing. He runs off, leaving me alone. I follow the path he's taken and notice a woman with a blue-lighted vest. She signals me to follow her; we walk up the nearest steps to another level. From here, we're able to see several people running around the first level.

"Wait here. I'll check around back," she whispers.

I position myself against the wall, waiting for her return. I see a shadow come up the stairs and aim my weapon at the entrance. This figure that appears in front of me also had a blue-lighted vest. He signals for me to head out. I find an opening near the side of the boulder and follow it. Once I make it inside, I see no one in sight. Where is Reece? He's probably on the lower level looking for me.

I continue walking through the maze. I hear footsteps behind me, so I begin to pick up the pace. While running, I hear the footsteps also speeding up, so I turn around to aim my weapon at the figure chasing me. Unable to make out each other's face, we both just stand there pointing our guns. He steps closer into the dim light, and there he is.

"Lower your weapon," my pursuer says.

There's no chance I'm going to let my guard down with him.

"How do I know you won't shoot?" I ask.

He grins as he begins to step closer.

"You don't."

He walks even closer until our weapons connect.

"I could've taken the shot if I wanted to," he says.

How? He was nowhere in sight for me to see him.

"I saw you when you were hiding behind the first boulder." Instead of shooting, he'd decided to follow me.

"Why not stop me there?" I ask.

He lowers his weapon and pushes his chest into mine.

"I wanted you to capture me."

There's no way. He wanted to wait for the perfect moment when we were alone to claim his victory.

"What's your next move?" he asks.

Before I can respond, the light on his vest begin to flash. I look behind him and notice the guy from earlier. Reece pushes my weapon to the side and runs off.

"Hey!" I follow him into a tunnel, trying to keep up. He is indeed quick. The opening is a closed-off field with just him and me. His light became solid again. I raise my weapon, prepared to shoot him. "No way out," I say with a grin.

He spins around and lowers his weapon.

"Any last words?"

He stops pacing and begins moving towards me. I start to take a few steps backwards. He walks faster, backing me into a corner. He grabs my weapon and tosses it to the floor. I attempt to make a run for my gun, but he kicks it out of view. I knock his weapon out of his hand. I begin running for my weapon again, but he collides with me and we fall onto the ground. After flipping each other over, I successfully pick up my gun, but as soon as I turn around, he attempts to grab it from me. We begin tugging the weapon back and forth. He's pretty intense, but I refuse to let go. We fall onto the ground again with him on top. I roll over, hoping to gain the upper hand. He turns me onto my side, and we both stand up, still pulling on the gun, until we are backed into a corner.

We just stand there breathing heavily.

"I see you're not going down without a fight," he manages to say in between breaths.

Now what do I do? Here I am backed into a corner. I guess my only strategy would involve tiring him out, and when he least expects it, attack.

"Likewise."

He stares into my eyes as if he's trying to read my mind. I try pushing him off, but my arms are exhausted. He smiles. He's probably figured out that I'm tired. However, he's not using force anymore, so he must be tired as well. I try gathering up enough strength one last time to push him off. Before I can act, his lips are pressed against mine. I don't move; what can I do in this moment? He grabs the back of my head and continues kissing me. *This shouldn't be happening. And why haven't I stopped him yet?* He pulls back, looking into my eyes, waiting for a response. I do the only thing I can think of. I push him, aim my weapon at his vest, and pull the trigger. His light begins to flash, and the music stops.

HELLO AWKWARDNESS

The ride back is deathly quiet. Neither of us knows what to say after the kiss. Maybe we're both overthinking it and can't say anything. I mean, we are building a friendship, right? It's not like we intended for this to happen, but then again, friends give each other kisses, don't they? I look over to see a blank expression on Reece's face. I wonder what's going on in his mind right now. Could he be just as confused as I am? He begins to turn his head towards me once he stops at the light. But I turn my head towards the window, looking outside, hoping to avoid his gaze. A stray dog sitting near the curb stares back at me. The look in its eyes is filled with sadness. I can't help but sympathize. What owner would abandon their pet like this? The sudden sound of thunder causes me to jump. The dog runs in the opposite direction of the traffic light. Part of me wishes I could run away with him. It's better than sitting here in awkward silence.

"Are you hungry?" Reece asks.

Part of me wants to say, "No, just take me back to my place," but another part of me wants to know why he kissed me. So, I nod my head yes. The light changes green, and he drives away from the intersection. Fifteen minutes later, we pull up to Yorkie's; they're known for serving brunch all day. One we're inside, I see that it's not too crowded. There's a booth near the window upfront, so we sit there. A server strolls over and brings us menus.

"Hi, my name's Stacie; I'll be back to take your drink order."

She goes to another booth near us to take an order. I reach for my phone after feeling a vibration. It's a voicemail from Riley.

"Cameron, I'm really sorry about earlier today. I know you're upset; I would be too if something like this were to happen to me. I'm sure you have so many questions. I really would like a chance to explain what's going on. Please call me."

I place the phone back into my pocket. What could she possibly say to me that would make sense of this? It's obvious she used me. She didn't feel the same way about me like I did about her.

"Are you okay?" Reece asks, interrupting my thoughts.

I shake my head no. Who would be ok feeling like this? The girl of my dreams humiliated me, and I possibly just lost my best friend. He grabs my hand, giving it a firm squeeze. I look down at his fingers gripping mine. Part of me wants to pull away, but I can't. He was only trying to comfort me. I should be thankful that he even cares about me.

Tears begin to well up in my eyes. I lay my head on the table to prevent Reece or anyone else here from seeing me like this. Why, just why? Why did I have to open up to her? Why did I have to fall for her? Why did I have to get involved with Leah and Anthony?

And why did Reece have to kiss me? It's just too much. He releases the grip on my hand and begins rubbing my back while I continue to cry. He stays quiet.

"Are you guys ready to order?" Stacie's back.

Reece asks for two waters and some tissues.

Okay, Cameron pull yourself together; you can't have a meltdown right now. I raise my head and begin wiping my face with my shirt. "I think I'll have a grilled cheese sandwhich," I croak. I force a smile to assure Reece that I am okay.

"What are you going to have?" I ask.

He grabs the menu and looks through it. After about two minutes, he decides on waffles with scrambled eggs and turkey sausage. A busboy drops off two glasses of water, and after Stacie confirms our order, she collects the menus and goes towards the kitchen.

"Did you enjoy the game?" Reece asks, looking at me with a sly grin. "I did. However, I wish it had been longer."

I don't agree. By the time we finished, I was tired, confused, and had worked up a serious appetite.

"So what did you think?' he asks.

"It was a workout, but fun," is all I can muster.

He tilts his head to the side while looking at me. What could he be thinking at this moment? I use a straw to take a sip of my water. He continues watching me with a blank expression.

I turn my head slightly, looking at the other tables to avoid his fixed stare. Out of the corner of my eye, I can still feel his gaze on me. His phone dings, and he begins reading his screen. Within seconds, his expression goes from blank to agitated. I continue watching him as he aggressively starts typing. I've never seen him upset before. This side of him frightens me. I wonder what has shifted his mood so quickly like this.

"Is something wrong?"

He doesn't respond. I try waving my hands to get his attention, but still no response.

"Reece?" Still nothing.

He continues typing on his phone with the same upset look on his face.

I reach out my hand to grab his wrist. He yanks his arm away, knocking his glass of water onto the floor, shattering it. The violent noise startles the customers nearby. I get up from the booth to kneel and pick up pieces of glass.

"Cameron, I'm sorry." He rushes to assist me with picking up the remaining pieces. With napkins from the table, I begin wiping the water and feel a sudden sharp pain.

"Oww!" My index finger starts to bleed. I grab another napkin and apply pressure to the wound.

"Let me take a look." Reece gently holds my arm and analyzes the damage. "It doesn't look like there's any glass in there."

I pull my hand back and head into the restroom where I run cold water over my finger.

After a few seconds, I grab a few pieces of paper towels to pat the cut dry. Who was he texting with? Out of nowhere, my ringtone echoes in the restroom and I pull out my phone to see Riley's name on the screen. I ignore the call. I'm not ready to hear any more lies from her. Just the thought of her voice is enough to get me upset. Reece bursts into the restroom. Once I see how concerned he is, my mood softens. Although I am upset about the kiss, I can't help but wonder what I could have done to provoke it. I've shown him kindness, but I've never made a move on him. All this time, Leah was right, but I guess I didn't want to believe it. He and I have been getting along so well and learning more and more about each other. Tears begin to flow from my eyes again. He grabs me into a hug and starts rubbing my head. I begin to embrace him tighter. To be honest, I don't know what I'd do if he weren't here.

I feel so lost; I'm not going to say I like this feeling; I wish it all would go away. If I had never met Riley, I wouldn't feel humiliated. I would be the same guy I was before—someone who enjoyed being in his comfort zone. Instead, I'm bawling my eyes out in a diner bathroom. We stay here for about ten minutes before someone knocks on the door. Then we hear Stacie's voice informing us our food is at the table. I can't even think about eating right now. I just want to crawl into bed and cry myself to sleep. It's better than being overwhelmed by so many emotions.

"I'm sorry about earlier; I received some upsetting family news from Ireland, but nothing for you to be concerned about."

"Can we leave?" I ask, releasing Reece.

He stares into my eyes and nods. I follow him into the dining room, but then go and wait outside as he talks to our server. The street isn't too busy at this time of night. After about two minutes, he returns with a couple of to-go containers and we get into his truck. Nearby, I see a sign indicating there's a city park at the next light.

"Can we stop there?" I ask.

"Sure thing."

Two minutes later, Reece pulls into the parking lot and I step out. A cool breeze is blowing.

"This feels nice." I walk towards a large field of grass and, once I reach the center, I lie down.

Reece follows me, lying in the opposite direction.

"When I was seven," I say, "my parents transferred me to a new school in Texas."

"How was that?"

"Terrifying." I force a laugh. "I didn't know what to expect; so many questions went through my head." My tears begin to flow. "I asked myself, will I make friends or enemies?" I wipe my eyes. "That first morning, my mom and dad were at the school to enroll me, and while we were waiting to see the principal, I had to use the restroom really badly, so I snuck out without my parents noticing."

"Rebellious, Cam," Reece laughs.

"I didn't make it to the restroom."

"How come?"

"There were two boys clearly wanting to give me a hard time." Reece turns on his side and gazes at me.

"I didn't want any trouble, so I tried to walk away. One of them pushed me and the other hit me."

Reece lies back down and scoots closer.

"Once I was on the ground, they both kicked me, but a girl's voiced called out, causing the two boys to run." I wipe my nose. "She helped me up and asked my name. She said those kids were just jerks and together we could protect each other from them."

"She sounds amazing."

"That same day at lunch, those two boys came back. They ate my lunch and poured milk on me. The young girl was nearby and threw her lunch at them. All four of us were sent to the principal's office."

"What happened?"

"The two boys got suspended. The girl's parents and mine became friends. And that's how Leah and I became best friends."

Silence fills the air.

"Whenever I was sad, she would lie next to me like you and I are now." I wipe my face trying to remove the tears. "She would place her cheek next to mine. She said it was a way to prevent my tears from falling."

More tears come as Reece scoots closer and places his cheek next to mine.

"There's also another cool way to prevent your tears from falling." I laugh at his response.

"And what might that be?"

"Run."

He stands and pulls me up.

"Come on." He runs towards the trail in the park and I start to follow.

"Hey, wait up!" I pick up speed and the wind fills my ears as I continue to sprint. My eyes are burning from more tears, but they blow away with the wind. I turn to my right and see Reece has dropped back and is running next to me.

HELLO MISTAKE

I must've been exhausted; I feel Reece tapping my shoulder and open my eyes to see him standing over me.

"Let's get you changed."

I look around and notice that I am not in my bed. I'm back at his place. I pull on my shirt to see I'm wearing the same thing. I look up at him, waiting for him to continue speaking.

"We were closer to my place."

He could've taken me back to my apartment. What if Leah's there waiting for me now. Wait a minute—I reach into my pocket and pull out my phone. There are no messages from Leah or Anthony. The time is 10:05 pm. Maybe I should call. Before I can press send to call Anthony, Reece grabs my phone.

"You were crying in your sleep; I didn't think it was a good idea to leave you alone."

"I need to check on Leah," I say, reaching back for my phone unsuccessfully.

He puts up a hand, signaling for me to stop.

"You're not going anywhere; you need to rest," he says sternly.

I plop back on the bed, feeling defeated. There's no way I can sleep now. Maybe once he's asleep, though, I could get my phone back. But by then, it may be too late. I have no choice but to wait until morning to call Anthony, so I just lie there. Reece stands there looking at me. He's only wearing those grey shorts, which leaves a generous view of his pecs and abs. He then crawls onto the bed and lies next to me.

"You will be okay."

He gives my arm a squeeze. How can he be so sure?

"I have something that can help."

He jumps up and walks out of the room. I continue looking up at the ceiling. Is this what heartbreak feels like? I've had two relationships in the past and never cried when they ended. I was actually relieved. There was Jennifer; she seemed to be more into her image than she was into me. Then there was Amber, a girl who enjoyed the finer things in life. Both split up with me using the same line: "It's not you. It's me." I guess it didn't bother me because I felt they were right. It wasn't me; I'm very involved when it comes to my relationships. My love language is based not just on emotions, but actions. Anyone can say anything, but it's what you do or what progresses in the relationship that maintains interest.

Reece walks back in with a bottle of wine in his hand. After the last round of drinks we had, I would think he understood alcohol was not for me. He sits on the floor and I do as well.

"What is this about?" I ask.

He pulls the cork off the bottle. "Let's play a game."

I'm not in the mood for games. I begin to stand up, and he pulls me down.

"The rules are simple."

Annoyed, I tilt my head to the side, waiting for him to continue.

"Just be open and honest."

"Fine, I'm honestly not interested in playing."

He shakes his head and grins.

"You start a sentence with, 'I think,' then take a sip," instructs Reece. "After that, you just say what you're thinking. And as you go along, the wine helps make it easier for things in your head to make it out of your mouth. You know the old saying, '*In vino veritas*'! I'll go first. I think…you're brave." He brings the bottle to his lips and takes a sip.

Brave? What about me says I'm brave? I couldn't even stand up to my best friend. He signals for me to start.

"I think…it's late," I say. Immediately after grabbing the bottle, I notice the aroma of the wine is strong. Why couldn't he bring anything other than this? I take a sip. The acidic taste takes me by surprise and I make a face. It's so strong and bitter. I wipe my lips. He covers his mouth to prevent himself from laughing at the response. Where's the water when you need it?

"I think…you're holding back." He takes a sip.

I am, holding back my frustration with this game. Why couldn't we just watch a movie and fall asleep? Is this what he calls cheering someone up?

"I think we should do something else." I grab the bottle and take a swig.

Thirty minutes later, my body is heavy. I lost count of how many sips I've taken of the wine, but the bottle is almost empty. Reece, however, seems just as awake as when we started the game.

"I think I'm done," I say, slurring over my words. A smirk forms at the corner of Reece's mouth; it seems that he's finding this game amusing.

"It ends once the bottle is empty," he declares.

I place both hands on my face squeezing my cheeks. I don't think I'll be able to finish this bottle with him.

"It's your turn to take a sip." He taps the bottle.

I snatch the bottle off the carpet and lift it to my lips. The taste doesn't seem to bother me as much anymore. I hand it back to him.

"I think you're a beautiful guy," he says before taking a sip.

His eyes never leave mine while he's drinking. I smirk at his response. What beauty does he see in me? He's the one with the good looks. He has an athlete's body, clear skin, and well-groomed hair that behaves.

"I think…you're delusional," I say, then take another sip. The weight of the bottle becomes lighter. There's just enough for one more sip. Good, then this game can finally be over.

"I think…you might surprise yourself," Reece declares, then downs the rest of the wine.

What does he mean by that? He grabs the empty bottle and walks into the bathroom. I follow him and stand in the doorway. I watch as he throws the bottle into the waste bin. He then grabs an unopened package with a toothbrush inside and opens it. It's blue and white. He looks through the medicine cabinet and pulls out toothpaste that he squeezes onto the toothbrush and then hands it to me. I walk further in, holding onto the counter to prevent myself from falling. He then picks up a grey and white toothbrush and applies toothpaste as well. We begin brushing our teeth together.

The scent of mint rushes through my nose and the taste mixes weirdly with the residual wine in my mouth. After a few minutes of that, he places cover caps on both toothbrushes and puts them onto the counter. He takes a step closer to me.

"There's some shorts there for you." I look behind me to see a navy-blue blue pair hanging off the doorknob. Where's the shirt? Before I can ask, he walks out of the bathroom and closes the door.

HELLO NEW DAY
Saturday

The sound of an alarm clock interrupts my sleep. I turn over to silence it. My head begins to throb. That's what I get for drinking all that wine last night. And now my stomach feels really unsettled. *Oh, no…* I jump out of bed and run into the restroom. I kneel next to the toilet and lift the seat cover. Within seconds, vomit is pouring out of me. This seems to be another side effect of a hangover? I wipe my mouth with the back of my hand and start rubbing my temples. The sound of birds chirping is coming through the window, so I cover my ears. Why does everything seem so loud? I stand up to look out the window, but instantly shield my eyes due to the sun beating in. I walk back into the bedroom and notice my phone on the nightstand. Reece must've put it here after he took it from me. There are still no missed calls or texts from Leah, but there is a message from Anthony.

"Hey, Cameron, Leah stayed the night. She left this morning before I woke up. I've tried calling her multiple times, but no answer.

If you hear back from her, please let me know. Also, no update on why she wanted to break up."

She still hasn't told him. Let's see if she'll pick up for me. I begin dialing her number. No answer, just straight to voicemail. I try calling again, but get the same result. Maybe I should call her mom, but then again I wouldn't want to upset Leah even more by getting her involved. I guess the only other option is to wait until she reaches out. I hope it's soon; I could use one of her hugs.

I step out of the bedroom, making my way down the hallway into the living room. Reece is standing in the kitchen making coffee. Noticing my presence, he looks up and waves. I step into the kitchen and watch as he finishes putting together his coffee. From my observation, it looks like he prefers it sweeter. There were numerous tastings in between the sugar and creamer. He pulls out a mug from the cabinet and slides it over towards me.

"I'm not a coffee drinker."

He rummages through a cabinet and hands me a packet. It's Earl Grey tea. I begin to open it, but he grabs it before I can finish. He retrieves a silver tea kettle and grabs a room-temperature bottle of water and pours it in. While turning the burner on, I notice a scar on his back. Why I didn't notice this at the club? It's pretty faded, and has probably been there for years.

"What happened there?"

I point to the lower part of his back; he turns around to see where my finger is pointing.

"I was very active."

He didn't answer my question entirely, but I can take a hint. He stands up straight and takes a sip of his coffee.

"I was protecting a loved one."

He places his cup on the counter.

"A few years ago, back in Ireland, there was a situation."

Which was?

"I was out with some loved ones at a pub." He spaces out.

"These guys were very loud and obnoxious, so we decided to move and sit somewhere else." *Okay.*

"In the midst of that, one of them grabbed her and wouldn't let go."

Her?

"I asked him to back off, but he shoved me."

Could he be referring to the woman in the picture?

"I shoved him back, the next thing I hear is glass breaking and screams; the guy and I were throwing punches and I felt a sharp pain in my back. His buddy stabbed me with a knife."

Silence fills the room.

"Sorry, I didn't mean…"

"You did nothing wrong."

He takes another sip of his coffee. "Anything else you're curious about?" He stares into my eyes.

"The tattoo?" I say.

He grins.

"It's a reminder."

"A reminder of what?" I question.

"When someone speaks it's important to be aware of their feelings in the moment." I follow his gaze towards the bookshelf in the living room.

This conversation seems to bring painful memories.

"Anyway, how are you this morning?" he asks.

Well, I'm not as emotional so that's a good start. "I'm feeling nauseous," I say, grabbing my stomach. Although there's a pounding in my head, feeling nauseated is what's bothering me the most.

He retrieves cold water from the refrigerator.

"Drink this until the water finishes boiling."

He removes the cap and hands it over.

"What do you have planned today?"

I was hoping to speak with Leah; it doesn't look like that might happen. I know for sure I can't go back to Anthony's. I'm afraid Leah might pop up and give me an earful. Maybe I should just go home and sleep the day away.

"Stay in bed," I respond before bringing the bottle of water to my lips for a very long swallow; the coolness is incredible refreshing. My body needed that hydration. By the time I place the bottle back on the counter, the water is half gone. I guess drinking alcohol does that to you.

"Hang out with me," Reece says after taking another sip of coffee.

We've already spent the night together, had a fun activity last night, and now we're chatting in the morning. What else could we possibly do today?

"I'll take you home so you can rest for a bit. Then I'll pick you up, let's say 5:00 pm?"

Part of me wants to say "No, I'd rather not." However, maybe it's better if I have a friend with me today. After all, it is Saturday; I should be out having fun.

"Okay," I respond.

The kettle starts to whistle. Reece removes it from the stovetop to place onto a potholder. He inserts the tea bag inside a mug and begins pouring the water. He then grabs a carton of coconut milk and adds that. He pulls out what looks like a small bottle of vanilla extract from the cabinet and squeezes a few drops into the mug followed by a tablespoon of coconut sugar. He hands the drink over to me. The aroma is subtle but amazing.

"What is this?" I blow into the cup, attempting to cool it down. I take just a small sip to ensure it won't burn my tongue. The milk from the carton helped cool it down a bit, so the temperature is just right.

"A London Fog Latte."

I take another sip, savoring the flavor.

"Thank you."

HELLO CONFRONTATION

After Reece drops me off, I decide to take a shower. Warm water falling against my skin feels very comforting right now. I enjoy using a bath sponge as opposed to a hand towel to scrub myself under the spray. The smoother surface feels more relaxing. I reach out to the sink counter to press play on the Bluetooth speaker and soon some very relaxing ambient music unobtrusively fills the room. I grab the body wash situated inside the shower and begin lathering it against my skin. The aroma of coconut and vanilla fills my nostrils. I've used a variety of scents, but this one is by far my favorite. After a few minutes of lathering, I place my entire body under into the jet spray; the water pressure is strong and very satisfying. Then I reach for the coconut milk shampoo and apply a small amount to my wet hair. I slowly massage my scalp. After a bit, I rinse out the shampoo and work in some conditioner and then wash that out. I spend another ten indulgent minutes in the shower before getting out. I wipe the steamed-up mirror. I stare at myself in the mirror; the person looking back at me is not someone I recognize.

"What's happening to me?"

I reach for some coconut hair mask located to the left of the counter and put a small amount in my hair. The cream is already thick; too much would leave clumps. So, I use the mirror to ensure I blend it all in. That's another thing I enjoy about my bathroom; the mirror and the spherical light fixtures that surround it. I wrap a towel around my waist and head towards my bedroom. The figure I see sitting on my bed causes me to yelp; I didn't expect to see her anytime soon, but here she is.

"Leah, I—"

She raises her hand, signaling me to stop, but doesn't say a word. I sit next to her in silence. There are so many things I want to say, but I'm not sure if my words could change what's happening now. I look over to Leah and watch as a tear rolls down her cheek.

"I'm so upset with you," she sniffles.

I lower my head, unsure of how to respond. Maybe I should stay quiet until she finishes speaking. She stands up and walks to the center of the bedroom.

"Why, Cameron?" She turns towards me.

The look on her face now is a mix between confusion and annoyance.

"I wanted to help."

This is true; I only wanted to take off some of the burdens she had. As her best friend, I thought she would understand that.

She places both hands on her forehead. "I didn't mention the pregnancy." She raises her hand again, in a preemptive move to silence me.

At this rate, I won't get a chance to share my side of the story. She seems to have made up her mind. It looks like I'm being painted as the villain. It seems pointless to talk to her, so I walk over to my dresser and begin looking for something to put on. I manage to find a light blue t-shirt, grab a pair of underwear, and head into the closet to retrieve a pair of jeans. I finish getting dressed in there.

"Leah, I'm sorry, I had good intentions," I say with some irritation in my voice.

She scoffs at me and walks out of the bedroom. I follow her.

"Where are you going?"

She is just inches away from the door. She turns around and walks right up to me.

"Away from here!" she yells and begins walking back towards the door.

"Leah, I'm—" before I can speak, she turns around with more tears streaming down her cheeks.

"Sorry!" she snaps and throws her hands in the air.

"Is that what you want to say?" I stand there in disbelief.

She's never raised her voice at me this way.

"I don't believe you, Cameron." She yanks the door open and storms out.

I close the door and lean my back against it. My eyes begin burning with tears and I let my body slide to the floor. This can't be it; this is not supposed to be how our friendship ends. There's no way we can't make it through this; we've been through so much and shared so much together. I pull out my phone and try calling her. Her phone rings three times before I'm sent to voicemail. I try again, but still no response.

I've got to catch up to her. I grab my keys from the kitchen counter, run out of my apartment, and lock the door behind me as quickly as possible. I run to the elevator, pressing the down button several times, hoping to speed it up. I'm on the fifth floor, but after a few seconds, I decide to take the stairs. I jump down them as fast as I can, hoping to catch Leah in the parking garage. Once there, I look around to see if I can spot her or her car. I ran through several aisles and still no Leah. I try calling her again, but still no answer. Crushed, I begin making my way back towards my apartment when my phone rings. It's Riley. I put the phone in my pocket and continue walking. I hear laughter around the corner, but it's just a female neighbor having a conversation on her phone. Then the sound of a car alarm startles me. It looks like some kids were throwing a ball that hit the back of someone's fancy foreign model. My phone rings again, but instead of pulling it out, I ignore it. I'm too drained to talk to anyone else now. I still haven't had a chance to calm down from my encounter with Leah, and Reece will be here in a little while.

I wasn't in much of a hurry to return to an empty apartment. Being too tired to walk it, I decide to take the elevator. Inside is a guy reading the paper. He peeps from behind the pages and smiles. I produce a weak smile in return. After a few seconds, I arrive on my floor. I wave goodbye and step out of the elevator. I turn down the hall to the left, walking towards the end where my apartment is located.

A familiar voice calls out my name.

I look up to see her standing at my door with a duffle bag in her hand. She's wearing pink shorts and a white top with her hair tied up.

"Can we talk?" Riley asks, approaching me.

There is no way for me to avoid her now.

HELLO TENSION

It hasn't even been twenty-four hours since I learned the truth about Riley and Mercedes. I haven't had much time to process what to say in the event we meet.

"Why are you here?" I ask, walking towards my door. As I start to unlock it, she grabs my shoulder and spins me around. Her beautiful eyes are looking right through me. She could've been my safe place: staring into her eyes and creating a wonderful life together. This could've been a beautiful beginning for the rest of our lives. Instead, I'm left with resentment. The girl I fancied, who was out of my league, has someone else.

"I have something to say to you," she begins. She looks at the floor then back at me. Why does she look so nervous?

"I left Mercedes."

My heart begins racing.

"Is it okay if I crash here?"

"Why would I let you stay here? You manipulated me."

She takes a step closer and grabs my hands. "I'm so sorry…I know I don't deserve to ask you for help, but I don't know what else to do."

I pull back my hands and fold my arms.

"Don't apologize unless you mean it," I shoot back.

"I do." She pleads.

"What exactly are you sorry for Riley?!" I shout. Her startled reaction makes me think that was too much. "Is it for not telling me, hurting me, or because you were caught?" I could send her out the door right now without having any regret. "Your breakup has nothing to do with me."

"Cameron. I'm…"

Putting her out won't solve anything, it may just make everything worst. "One night," I say. It's as much charity as I can muster before falling onto the couch. "I'll give you one night to decide whatever you want to do."

"Thank you."

I watch as Riley unpacks her duffel bag. Inside it, she has a few items to last her a week. The fight between her and Mercedes was about their differences, she says, and mentions that over the past few months several issues kept coming up over and over again. Some of them were smaller than others, but it was becoming too much for her to handle. Why did she choose to come here? There's nothing I can do to make her situation better. But as painful as it is for me to see her, I couldn't turn her away. In my eyes, she's still this sweet girl who's a perfect match for me.

"Is it okay if I put this stuff in the bathroom?" she asks, holding a few hair products.

I nod my head yes while pointing to where it's located. I hear an alert from my cell phone—it's Reece.

"Just checking in and wanted to know how you're doing. I'll see you soon." His text ends with a hugging emoji. It makes me warm, knowing I have a friend who cares. That said, I'm unsure if I'll be able to hang out with him today due to Riley's arrival. I begin typing. "Hey Reece, I'm ok.

Thanks for checking in. However, I'll have to take a raincheck today. Something's come up."

Riley appears back in the living room.

"Do you have anything to eat?" she asks, rubbing her stomach.

I haven't had a chance to go grocery shopping lately. I do have some cheese and crackers she could snack on. Her stomach actually begins to growl audibly; I think she'll need more than that.

"We can go out and grab something," I suggest.

She nods in agreement. After deciding to take my car, Riley mentions how she's enjoyed going to Taco Mania every weekend, so that's where we head. I've never been, but the reviews for this simple food truck located in a shopping plaza are good.

Once we're there, a cashier waves as we walk up, but she's assisting a customer ahead of us, which gives me time to look over the menu printed on the side of the truck. Riley wants the Chicken Mania with shredded chicken, garlic sauce, feta cheese, and parsley. I decide to take a chance on the Seafood Mania, which has shrimp, crawfish tails, and crab. When it's our turn, we each order one taco and a lemonade. Probably out of guilt, Riley pays for the meal and collects a ticket with a bold number "53" printed on it. Next to the truck are five tables with benches. We sit at the closest one to make sure we hear our number. She tilts her face towards the sun and stretches her arms.

"It's so beautiful out today," she says, reaching for the blue sky.

I agree. There might be a few clouds in the sky, but the abundant sunshine has lit up everything. I watch as she tucks a brown curl behind her ear.

"Thank you," she says quietly.

I glance over to see her looking at me. Why is she thanking me? I should thank her for buying me lunch.

"For what?" I ask.

"Giving me a place to stay."

Her eyes begin to water. Although I'm upset about what happened between us, I feel bad for her. Going through a bad breakup can be overwhelming.

"You're welcome. Thanks for lunch."

Although I would like a real explanation, maybe just having her around could provide some closure.

"Order number fifty-three," a voice yells from the truck.

"That's us." Riley quickly gets up to collect our food.

I pull out my phone to check the time; it is now 2:25 PM. I didn't realize Reece had texted back. I read his message: "There's no way I'm letting you bail on me. I'll pick you up at 4 PM." That's an hour earlier than we had discussed. What do I do now? I don't think it's good to leave Riley alone. I also don't want Reece to feel slighted. He's been so supportive and kind.

"Eat up," Riley says, setting a plate in front of me. She brought some condiments as well as chips and salsa.

"This looks great," I say, eyeing the food. I take a bite of my taco. It's filled with so much flavor; I can taste butter, different types of herbs, and the seafood. Riley begins dressing her taco using a variety of salsa-filled dipping cups. She hands me one filled with green salsa. I apply a small amount on my taco and take another bite; the salsa definitely adds extra spice. I take a sip of the lemonade; it's not too sweet. There are also bits of fresh mint leaves floating inside. Everything about this meal is perfect.

"What do you have planned today?" she asks, taking a sip of her lemonade.

After another swallow of my drink, I reply, "Reece is picking me up." Her expression changes; she almost seems hurt.

"You're welcome to join us."

Suddenly, her face lights up with excitement. Now how should I tell Reece?

An hour or so later, as Riley and I pull back into my parking garage, I see Reece's truck. He's not sitting inside it, so I assume he's at my front door.

Waiting for the elevator, Riley asks me, "So, who is this Reece guy?"

"He's a friend; you met him that night at the night club," I respond.

"Oh, the bartender." She punches my arm playfully.

Once the elevator arrives, we step inside. The ride up is filled with silence; it seems like neither of us knows what to say. When the doors open, Reece appears and embraces me in a hug.

"Cam, where'd you go?"

"We went to grab something to eat," I reply nervously.

He releases the hug and stares at me with both hands gripping my shoulders.

"I ate a taco."

He turns towards Riley; I notice his jaw clenching.

"Hi, we met before." She extends her hand.

Reece continues to stare without saying anything or returning her greeting. After a few seconds, she drops her hand.

"Umm, I think we should get out of the elevator." I head towards my apartment and, once I start to go inside, I turn to see Riley and Reece glaring at each other.

"Come on in."

They begin walking and, upon making it to the door, they bump into each other. Reece takes a step back, allowing Riley to enter. Once inside, Reece sits down on the couch and stretches his arms along back of it. Riley sits across from him and folds her arms. Neither of them says a word.

"Would you guys like something to drink?" I ask, looking between the two.

"No!" they both reply immediately. I shuffle into the kitchen and grab a bottle of water for myself. *Okay, Cameron, what now?*

The tension is thick. Reece wants to hang out, but Riley is going through a difficult time. What could we all do that would make them both happy? I know Reece had something planned, but in case it doesn't go over well with Riley, I might need a backup option. There's the zoo, a park, a dinner cruise. *Oh, wait, biking—that's it!* We can go bike riding. I make my way back towards the living to find them in the exact same positions. They both look at me.

"Would either of you want to go bike riding?"

"Yes," says Riley.

"No," says Reece. "I figured you and I would go zip lining," he counters.

Zip-lining? Is there any activity he knows that doesn't involve being so high up? We already went rock-climbing.

"I've never been," I respond.

I look to Riley, who seems to like the idea.

"Cameron, you'll enjoy it. The feeling is fantastic," she says excitedly.

Well, I guess that's settled.

37

HELLO CONFLICT

The zip-lining center is massive. Hanging from the ceiling are metal fixtures in the shape of buckles. The floor is constructed of black and white marble and looks like it's polished every day; I can see my reflection. Behind the front counter is a safety list of dos and don'ts. Glancing around, there are so many people, including a lot of teenagers. How can they be so calm? I watch as Riley and Reece head over towards the counter. It looks as if they're trying to figure out who's going to pay. I'm not interfering, because I don't want to be in the middle. That said, I don't really want to be here at all.

In the center of the building is a kiosk with pictures and a monitor showing videos of other guests in action. I click "play" and a young woman is shrieking as she goes lower and lower towards the ground. Another one is of a boy screaming at the top of his lungs. Some of the pictures are group shots of guests looking a little scared. I feel a tap on my right shoulder and turn around to see Riley standing there.

"Reece is paying for our tickets, so I figured I'd check to see how you're doing."

Terrified—what's so fun about falling twenty or thirty feet to the ground?

"I'm fine."

I want to run outside immediately and hide; get as far away from this place as I possibly can. A knot begins to form inside my stomach. *It's okay, Cameron; it'll be fine. All you have to do is close your eyes when you jump off.* Riley touches my face with the back of her hand. I cringe a little due to the coolness.

"Are you sure you're okay?" she asks again. "You feel a little warm."

I nod my head yes.

"Ahem," interrupts Reece. "Let's go." He hands over our tickets.

Riley and I follow behind as he begins making his way over to the concierge.

"Hello, I'm George. How many?"

Reece holds up three fingers. George removes a rope for us to walk through the door and now we are outside on a path with green arrow markers on it. While following them, I hear a scream coming closer. I quickly glance up and see someone speeding on a zipline right above us.

Okay, there's no way I'm doing this. I spin around, and Reece grabs my arm.

"Come on," he says, pushing me in front of him.

Once we reach a gate, a clerk collects our tickets and requests we stand behind the nearest guests, two older gentlemen. They sincerely look thrilled.

"My wife and I brought our grandson here last summer!" exclaims one of them.

Shrieks fill my ears once again. I look up to see a figure approaching the ground. *That's it.*

I'm out of here. I turn around, but Reece is blocking my way.

"Don't even think about it," he says.

Standing back near the gate, Riley is having a conversation on her phone. She's far enough away that I can't make out what she's saying, but she is clearly frustrated. I wonder if she's talking to Mercedes.

"What's wrong?" asks Reece.

I turn back towards the gate. He places his arm around my shoulder.

"You'll be fine."

I shrug his arm off. Of course, he'd say that. He's used to this kind of stuff. The attendant opens the gate for the two older gentlemen to pass through. The ominous clank of it closing startles me. We're next.

"This is going to be great," says Riley, suddenly standing next to me. I didn't hear her approach. I watch as her hair blows in the wind. I know I should be over my feelings for her, but I can't help it. Every time I look at her, so many emotions surface back up. My heart just beats faster when she's near.

"Are *you* okay?" I ask. She runs her fingers through my hair and nods her head yes. I can tell she's feeling uneasy after the phone call.

The gate opens, and my heart begins to race. I freeze in place; this is about to happen. My chest tightens, and I struggle to breathe. I place my hands over my heart, then on my thighs. I edge forward and begin to take deep breaths in and out. I feel a hand on my back.

"Cam?" Reece calls out. I turn my head and he stares into my eyes.

The gate closes.

"We don't have to do this."

I drop to my knees and start breathing in and out. Reece joins in. My breathing begins to slow down. He grabs both of my hands and rubs them.

"Just say so, and we'll leave."

After a few seconds, we stand up together slowly.

"Let's go." I can barely get the words out.

He pulls me, walking back towards the entrance we came from. I stop.

"I'm okay now," I say in between breaths. I don't want to ruin this moment for him or Riley.

They both seemed really excited to come here. Now I'm the one pulling him back towards the gate. The attendant opens it again, and we continue to walk, with Riley leading the way this time. I can hear birds chirping as we get closer to the stairwell. Riley goes up first. Then I place my right foot on the first step…

"Cam?"

I spin around to face Reece. A huge smile appears across his face. I do my best to return one and continue making my way up the stairs. Once I reach the top, a middle-aged woman with a name tag reading "Sandra" hands us lanyards, carabiners, pulleys, and trolleys to put on for safety. I memorize what was needed from the list earlier. There's some weight to it, but nothing I can't handle. After several failed attempts attempting to secure mine, Riley comes over. She laughs as she adjusts my harness. She seems to be in a better mood.

"Are you feeling better?" she asks.

I nod my head yes as she ensures my harness is secured. I put on my helmet, but have trouble connecting the safety straps. Riley helps me.

As I pull on my gloves, I notice an agitated look on Reece's face. He becomes aggressive as he's putting on his gear. I walk over and place a hand on his shoulder.

"Need some help?" I ask while laughing. He looks up, and the expression on his face softens.

"No, I got it."

We walk over to Sandra and listen as she goes over the rules. The wind is blowing, so it's a little difficult to hear some of what she is saying.

"Are there any questions?" she asks.

After a few seconds with no response from us, we head over to the wire. I watch as the instructor secures Riley onto the connector. There are so many clicks before she gives the thumbs up. Riley turns around and waves. I wave back, and within seconds she just jumps. No hesitation at all. She glides through the air, screaming with excitement. Next up is Reece. He seems much more worried about me than his own safety. I give his shoulder a firm squeeze and force a smile onto my face to let him know I'll be okay. Once he's secured, he looks back and gives me a thumbs up. A moment after I return it, he jumps.

Then the instructor signals for me to come over… My heart starts pounding in my chest. As I walk over towards the ledge, I wonder how long it will take before making it to the ground.

What if I get stuck in the middle of the line in mid-air? I take a step back; the instructor looks at me quizzically.

"Give me a moment," I say, spinning around to pull myself together. I inhale and exhale slowly, trying to find some calm. *Okay, Cam, you can do this. There's nothing to be afraid of. Reece* and Riley are right below, waiting for you. As long as you follow the instructions, you'll be great.

I return to the ledge.

"How are you feeling?" Sandra asks.

I glance down over the edge, and my heart is still beating very fast. I take another step back, looking at Sandra.

"A little nervous."

Come on, Cam, you got this. I start jumping up and down a little, hoping it'll help with the nerves.

"Okay, I'm ready."

She secures my harness onto the latch and then gives me a thumbs up.

"Any last words?" she asks.

"What?" I asked, shocked.

She winks and without any warning, shoves me. I hear someone scream like they're being murdered and then realize it's me. The wind against my face is a serious rush, but I begin to feel nauseous. I close my eyes, hoping it'll help diminish some of the fear. Instead, it freaks me out even more. I continue screaming as I glide through the air. After a few seconds, I open my eyes to see two figures coming closer into view. It's Reece and Riley. My speed begins to decrease the nearer I get to them. Once I finally land, Reece rushes over to remove the harness.

"How was it?!" Riley asks, appearing behind him.

"Eye-opening."

38

HELLO DRAMA

We decide to grab some ice cream after zip-lining. As I'm driving, I look in the rearview mirror and see Riley texting in the backseat. She has the same agitated look from earlier. Out of the corner of my eye, I notice Reece in the front seat texting away. The ride from zip-lining has been totally silent. I want us to bond, but I don't want it to be forced.

"So, did everyone enjoy zip-lining?" I ask with as much enthusiasm as I can muster after that death trap of a ride.

"Yeah!" they respond in unison, but then instantly turn back to their phones. I switch on the radio and electronic dance music jumps out of the speakers. It reminds me of the night out at the club with Reece. Ten minutes later, we arrive at Freezies a local ice-cream shop. Inside, the menu hanging from the ceiling is crammed with dozens of flavors.

"My treat—what flavor do you guys want?" I ask with enthusiasm, hoping to shift the mood.

Like me, they both need more time to decide. I notice other smaller sub-sections of the menu; they have gelato and full-on sundaes here, too. So many choices; it's been a while since I had a sundae. Maybe I should go with that. Hold on; there are also floats.

"I'll go with the triple chocolate bowl," says Riley.

"And I'll have the caramel surprise," Reece adds.

"Okay, you two go find a seat, and I'll be right there," I say.

After placing the order, an alert from my phone indicates I have a text. It's from Anthony: "Hey Cameron, I hope all is well. Have you heard from Leah? She still hasn't responded to any of my messages today."

Yeah, I have heard from her; the last time we spoke was earlier today before she stormed out of my apartment. I begin typing. "Yes, earlier today. We didn't get to discuss much." I place my phone back in my pocket once our order shows up. I collect the tray and make my way through the very crowded parlor. Once I reach the empty chair between Riley and Reece, I set the tray down.

They are both staring at their phones with blank expressions. I hand each of them their ice cream. When I sit, neither of them looks up. I eat a spoonful of my sundae; the taste of vanilla and chocolate tingles my senses. At least there's that.

"This is so good," I say, pointing at my sundae.

Still no response from either of them.

I continue eating. After a few more scoops, I decide some serious action—or something silly—is required to get their attention. I dip both of my index fingers into the whipped cream and smear some on both their cheeks. They look up and look confused. I begin to laugh at the expressions on their faces, which provokes them to laugh at my reaction.

"You're a funny guy," Riley says, wiping the whipped cream from her cheek.

Reece does the same.

"How did you two meet?" she asks, waving a finger between Reece and me.

"At a clothing store," I reply. I go in for another spoonful of my sundae.

"How did you two?" asks Reece while staring coolly at Riley.

After a few awkward seconds, I jump in.

"At a yogurt shop."

Mellow out, Reece, please. He's usually kind and talkative. I nudge his shoulder as he continues staring at Riley. He looks at me then puts a spoonful of ice cream in his mouth. "What's after this?" I ask, stirring my sundae a bit.

Neither of them say anything. Again, with the silence. Maybe we should end this hangout session today; it's evident that these two are not going to get along anytime soon.

"Let's play a game," Reece responds jovially.

I don't trust that tone, but okay, a game, that's a start; an ice breaker. I like that.

"The rules are simple. You start your sentence with 'I don't.'" *Wait… No, no, no, no-no.*

"Or, we could play something else!" I interject.

He and Riley both look really tense again. I put my head on the table; I desperately want to disappear at this moment. My crush and my new friend look as if they want to tear each other apart.

"Okay," Riley says, staring at Reece.

I lift my head with a pleading look for her not to participate in this. This is not going to end well for any of us.

"I'll start," says Reece. "I don't like...manipulation." He announces this while staring at Riley.

"I don't like...judgment," responds Riley, who stares back. "You're turn, Cameron."

"I don't want to play," I reply.

"I don't like liars," Reece continues.

Riley smiles, then replies, "I don't like jerks."

I lay my head back on the table.

"I don't like ulterior motives," Reece says.

"I don't like assumptions," Riley counters.

Can we end this already?

"I don't like you," says Reece.

"And I don't like you!" Riley yells.

I jolt up and out of my seat. "That's it! I don't like this game," I shout and head into the restroom. I can't believe these two. As I look at my reflection, so many thoughts begin running through my mind. I wanted to enjoy a day with no drama. Instead, I'm here watching them go at each other. I turn on the faucet, place both my hands in the sink, and splash water on my face. If only I could sneak out and leave. There's not even a window in here to crawl through. But I couldn't do that since I drove them both here. I pull out my phone. Still no response from Anthony. He's probably going through it just like I am. I wish I could call Leah and vent. I'm sure I'm the last person she wants to hear from now. But we've been through a lot and I'm not giving up on our friendship. We have a strong bond. We'll make it through this. It's a setback.

I dial her number and the phone rings a few times before going to voicemail. "Leah, call me back; we need to talk."

HELLO REGRET

When I come out of the restroom, I don't see Riley and Reece at the table. I look around, assuming they might've switched seats. Still no sign of them. Where could they have gone? I go outside; maybe they're at the entrance or sitting on the little patio. When I can't find them anywhere, I begin to panic. I call Riley's phone, but get sent to voicemail. Then I call Reece, and after the second ring, he picks up.

"I'm standing near the car."

I run over then and see Reece leaning on the passenger door, but there's no Riley. Where could she have gone?

"What happened?" I ask confused.

"She left."

Yeah, I can tell, but why? As if reading my mind, he lets me know.

"We said some things to each other." *Things like what?*

"I think it's best if you and I talk somewhere else."

I unlock the car door and once we're sitting inside, I wait for Reece to give me some answers. He looks at me irritated. I'm the one who should be upset. What was supposed to be a fun day has turned into a pretty crappy one.

"What happened?" I demand.

He secures his seatbelt and sits there.

"Reece!"

Still no response.

I fasten my seatbelt and start the car. He places his hand on my arm. I glance over to see hurt in his eyes.

"What happened?" I ask with a softer tone.

"I don't trust her," he admits.

I wait for him to continue.

"My gut is telling me she's not a nice person."

What could he think she's hiding? She made it very clear that she's not into me.

She told me about her and Mercedes.

"Reece, look she…"

"No excuses," he says, looking straight ahead.

"What has gotten into you?"

I don't like this side of him. Could it be possible he's upset that I invited her or is it about the kiss we shared? Maybe if I knew, I could help fix whatever issue it is first.

"Drive," he says without looking at me.

I shift the gear into reverse and speed out of the parking lot.

The drive to his house is filled with silence. Reece falls asleep halfway through. After we arrive at his place, he exits the car without even a goodbye. I try calling Riley several times, but still no answer. I even send her a text while I wait inside my parking garage. Can this day get any worse?

I ride the elevator up to my floor. Once I exit, I see Riley sitting on the floor, her head against the door. She looks as if she's been crying. Once she sees me, she stands up. I race over towards her and embrace her in a hug. It really hurts me knowing she's sad. We stand in each other's arms for some time. Finally, she releases my hug and looks me in the eye.

"Cameron, I have something to say. I'm so sorry for not explaining my relationship with Mercedes. There's so much about her and me you should know."

I'm not interested in knowing about their past; I'm interested in learning how she feels now.

"I like you."

I gasp at these words coming from her mouth. She likes me! I'm so unable to contain my joy that I pick her up and swing her around. I'm so happy to hear her say it. It validates that I wasn't in this alone. The feelings I have for her mean something. She laughs in excitement once I put her back onto the ground.

"I—"

I put my index finger over her lips before she can speak again. I want to enjoy this moment—the moment that my beautiful crush confessed her feelings for me.

"Thank you," I say quietly.

She moves my hand and places her warm lips on mine; it feels so natural. She wraps her arms around my neck as we linger in this moment. Her kiss calms me; all the doubt and nervousness fade away. I don't notice until we stop to catch our breath that tears are rolling down my cheeks. She wipes them away and pulls me into another hug. I don't want this moment to end. I know I can't completely erase everything that has happened and there are still unanswered questions about her relationship with Mercedes, but I can try my best to get past it all. Now if only I could work on my relationship with Reece. He's been my biggest support. I don't want to seem selfish; his feelings are just as real as mine. Could it be possible he feels the same way about me like I do for Riley?

My phone vibrates in my pocket. I pull it out to see Leah's name.

"Hello," I say, waiting anxiously for a response.

"Come over," she says and ends the call.

Why did she have to call at this exact moment? I should just ignore her and meet up when

I'm ready; that's what she's been doing. Then again, this fight has lasted long enough.

HELLO UNFRIENDED

I knock on the door, waiting for Leah to answer. After the second knock, the door opens. She walks away and takes a seat. I step in, shutting the door behind me. I glance around her apartment and notice a lot of tissues all over the place. There are also empty snack packages lying around. I sit next to her, but she gets up and stands in the center of the floor. Placing both hands on her hips, she begins to pace. I sigh in annoyance. How will we ever get this resolved if she can't even stand to be near me?

"Leah."

No answer.

I call her name again, but she stays silent. I shake my head in agitation and get off the couch.

"Is this how you're going to behave every time I see you?!" I shout.

She looks at me angrily. "Don't turn this around on me!" she yells back.

I'm not turning anything around on you. Maybe if you stop acting like a child, we could have a conversation and get through this.

I try to soften my tone. "I'm not. I just want to have a civilized conversation." She folds her arms while staring at me.

"I made a mistake," I continue. "It was wrong to go behind your back." I sit back down on the couch. "I'm sorry."

She takes a seat across from me. "Why?" she asks after a few seconds of silence. "Why did you?"

I lower my head. "I wanted to help." She scoffs at my response.

"You both were in pain, and I thought I could help ease some of it." She scoffs again and I begin to get agitated. Does she even care?

"Do you think it's okay to be selfish?" I ask, annoyed. I raise my head to see her glaring at me.

"Selfish?" she says, raising her voice. "What's selfish is you not caring about how I might've felt." She walks into the kitchen and I stand up to follow.

"I did care. Maybe too much. I evaluated a lot of scenarios of what I thought might happen and a lot of them turned out badly."

She grabs a bottle of wine and a fills a glass up halfway.

"What I didn't suspect is my best friend being unreasonable," I continue.

She takes a sip of wine. "Unreasonable, you say." She laughs. "I think your lack of consideration is unreasonable." She slams the glass on the counter. "You were so wrapped up and delusional about a girl."

What?

"Cameron, did you ever think to ask me what I want? No, you didn't, you assumed." She takes another sip of wine.

"That's unfair," I reply and slam my hand on the counter. "I consoled you as much as you allowed."

She walks back into the living room and I follow.

"I don't understand, Leah; why are you like this?"

She places the wine glass on the coffee table and walks closer towards me. "You're selfish, that's why!" she shouts.

When have I ever been selfish? Since we were young, I've been there for her, probably more than I have for myself. Where is this coming from?

"Have you ever thought about what's going through *my* mind, Cameron?" I say nothing.

"No, because you were too busy worried about others."

This is outrageous. I've been worried about her this entire time.

"I disagree—"

She waves her hand, signaling me to stop. "You were so focused on your crush."

"Leah—" As I begin to speak, she walks back towards the table to have another sip of her wine and then interrupts me.

"Not only that, but you were also hanging out with some guy more than with me." She takes another sip. "I don't think I can do this anymore."

"Do what?"

"This!" she points between her and me.

"I don't like this either, Leah; us fighting like this. Can't we go back to the way things were when we were younger?" I say, walking closer to her.

I place my hands on her shoulder and, for a moment, I can see in her eyes how desperately she wants us to make up too. I embrace her in a hug; tears begin to stream down my cheeks. Then she begins to sob. After a few seconds of embracing, we step apart.

"We're not kids anymore, Cam," she says in between sniffles. She wipes her face with her right hand while the left one is placed on her hip. We stand there in silence, neither of us knowing what else to say. I spin around and walk towards the door. Once I open it, she grabs my arm. I turn around. Her eyes are red, and tears begin flowing again.

"I think we should take a break," she says softly. She then covers her mouth with her hand.

Those were not the words I wanted to hear. I never imagined us ever coming to this point. This is hard to swallow; I'm losing my best friend. My heart skips a beat, and I struggle to breathe. I fall to the floor, placing my head on my knees with my arms wrapped around my legs. Leah kneels and hugs me.

"I love you, Cam; but maybe it's time for us to figure out our own lives."

I don't want this. You hear about friendships ending, but I don't want this to happen to us. I start crying harder; I feel as if I can't breathe. I begin to hyperventilate. She rubs my back and places her head onto mine.

HELLO BABY

Leah and I spent thirty minutes just crying on the floor before I left. I decide to go for a drive, hoping that will help clear my mind. It's only made things worse, so I decide to head over to Reece's. Although we left on rocky terms, he is the only other person I can think of to calm me. I try calling him a few times before going over, but he doesn't answer the phone. Ten minutes later, I receive a call from Jessie. I pick up and hear him breathing heavily.

"Jessie, what's wrong?"

In the background, I hear someone scream.

"Jessie, what's going on?"

And then there's loud thud from the other end of the line.

"Cameron, it's happening," he says with some panic in his voice.

What is he talking about? Oh wait, it's happening.

"Where are you?" I ask.

"At home, trying to get everything in the car."

"I'm on my way" I say and take the nearest exit.

"No, meet us at Johnson's Hospital." He hangs up.

Thirty minutes later, I manage to make it there. Jessie didn't pick up or return my calls during that time, so I'm not sure which floor or room they're in. I run to the reception desk, but there's a couple in front of me asking too many questions. I stand in line for five minutes, waiting for them to finish. Another receptionist appears on the opposite end of the desk. I run over as soon as she calls "Next."

"Hi, my friend and his wife are here having a baby. Jessie and Amber Jones."

Without responding, she continues typing on her keyboard. After a few seconds of silence, she looks up.

"They're on the third floor."

I sprint to the nearest elevator.

Apparently, a lot of people are using the elevator, because it's taking forever to arrive. I decide to use the staircase and run up three flights. When I reach the third floor, my phone starts ringing. It's Jessie.

"Hey, I'm on your floor. What room?"

I look one way down the long hallway and then the other and see Jessie waving his hand. I run in his direction. I hug him as soon as I'm near.

"I'm about to be a dad." His face lights up as he says those words.

"You sure are, buddy," I say, shaking his hand. "What is the latest with Amber?"

"Well, the pain went down a bit," he replies, looking around. "And my mom and dad should be here soon."

An hour later, his parents arrive. They're just about the most loving people I've ever met. They hug me as if I am their own. Jessie is inside the delivery room with Amber when they arrive.

"Do either of you want something to eat or drink?" I ask.

"A bottle of water would be great," says his mom. "Thank you very much."

On my way over to the vending machine, I see I've gotten a text from Riley. "Hey Cameron, I hope you're ok." She sent a picture of herself sitting on the couch with popcorn. I respond with a blank face emoji. I have mixed feelings right now. Part of me is sad due to losing my friendship with Leah, part of me is happy right now for Jessie and his wife and their imminent baby, but the other part of me is still questioning my reality in general.

I put my phone back into my pocket. I decide on peanuts for a snack and select three bottles of water. Walking back to the waiting room, I find Jessie sitting in a chair alone.

"Hey, how is Amber?" I ask, handing him a bottle of water.

He twists off the cap and takes a sip. "She's more comfortable now; my parents went inside."

I open the peanuts and pour some into both of our hands.

"Thanks for being here," he says, eating some peanuts.

"You're more than welcome. And both of you will do great," I assure him.

Twenty minutes later, he goes back inside the room with Amber and his parents. I sit there listening to music on my phone. I lose track of time because when I look up, it's already 7 pm. I've been here for three hours. Anthony and his parents are still inside, so I get up and poke my head through the door.

"Hey, how's it going?" I look over at Amber, who gives me a welcoming smile.

"Cameron, thank you for coming," she says.

"I'm very happy to be here." I look over to Jessie.

"Baby will be here soon," he says. "I'll call you when it happens. Go home and get some rest, bud."

"That's okay; I'll be out here if you need me." I go back into the hallway and take a seat.

"Hey, you."

I look up to see a guy in scrubs with orange hair standing there. I instantly stand up once I recognize his face.

"You're the guy from the club."

I glimpse at his name tag. "Alex"

"I am, and you are…?"

"Cameron."

He extends his hand and we shake.

"Oh yeah, now I remember. What brings you in?" He flips through charts on a clip board.

"Expecting a baby."

He raises an eyebrow and places the clipboard behind his back. He tilts his head to the side.

"Baby, huh? Congratulations"

I wave my hands in front of me. "It's not mine, it's my friend's, she's due any minute now."

"Oh, for Mr. and Mrs. Jones? I'm their nurse."

A scream alarms us and we run into the room. Jessie's dad has his arm around his mom and Jessie is holding Amber's hand.

"It's happening!" he shouts.

Alex leaves the room quickly to get the doctor.

"What can I do to help?" I ask, panicked.

"Walk mom and dad out."

I go over to help Jessie's dad with his mom. Once we're in the hallway, a doctor in a white coat struts ahead of Alex into the room, followed by two other medical personnel. After two hours, Ambers screams are suddenly replaced by the cries of a baby. The staff who helped with the delivery leave the room and let us inside. Jessie is holding the baby while Amber, exhausted, lies there watching.

"It's a girl," Jessie softly announces and starts gently dancing her around the room in his arms.

"Congratulations to you both," I say.

His parents step back into the room and gather around them.

"I'll let this moment soak in for you all. Jessie, call me if you need anything."

I wave goodbye to everyone and head towards the elevator. It arrives more quickly than the last time and inside is a man with his own little one. I wave to the little baby as I step into the elevator and the dad smiles at me.

I pull out my phone once again to call Reece. He answers on the third ring.

"Hey, is it okay if I come over?"

My question is greeted with silence on the other end.

"Reece, are you there?"

"Yes, I think it's time. See you soon." He hangs up.

What does he mean by time? Is there something he has to say, as well? Maybe I'll finally get some answers from him. Stepping out of the elevator on the first floor, I get a call from Riley.

"Hello?" Static fills my ears. "Riley, can you hear me?" I run outside the hospital, but by then the call has dropped. I dial back, but there's no signal. Once inside my car, I try calling her again, but it goes straight to voicemail. I start the car and anxiously start the trip over to Reece's place.

42

HELLO CONFESSION

The lights outside his place are bright. I stroll towards the steps. My heart begins to race in my chest. Why am I so nervous? I've tried to imagine so many scenarios in my head on how this would go. In the first one, he yells at me for forgiving Riley so quickly. In the second, he asks me to choose between friendship with him or dating Riley. In the last scenario, he asks never to see me again. All those concepts are intense, but I hope none of them come to pass. I so value the bond we've developed. It would kill me to lose another friend.

I knock on his door. After a few seconds, Reece is standing in front of me in a tank top and shorts. I give a smile and wave. Instead of returning either gesture, he opens the door further. I walk in and smell the scent of sandalwood. There's an empty bottle of wine sitting on the kitchen counter. *What is it with all this wine?* I turn around to get a look at his face, but he's expressionless and completely unreadable. I take a seat on the sofa, waiting for him to sit as well. Instead, he stands with his back against the front door, watching me.

His voice breaks through the silence. "What is it you want to say?"

When he speaks, he almost sounds angry. I lean forward, placing my elbows on my knees.

"Today wasn't what I expected," I begin. "You didn't seem like yourself." He folds his arms and continues staring at me.

"Did I do something wrong?" I ask.

"What do you think?" he says, raising his voice.

It startles me as it echoes inside the living room.

"I think you're bothered by something, and I would like to know what it is," I respond.

He pushes himself off the door and walks towards the center of the room.

"You're right. I am bothered," he says. "I'm upset with myself." What does he have to be upset with himself about?

"I've asked myself over and over: why?" *Why? What?*

"I like someone who doesn't even notice," he continues.

I can understand his pain. That's how I felt about Riley, but what does this have to do with me? That's no excuse to act the way he did today. This can't just all be about a kiss. He even took his frustration out on Riley.

"It sucks to hold in feelings for someone, but today…" He rushes over to me with his face inches from mine. "Today was horrible. And you want to know what's even worse?"

I'm not sure if I should answer or nod my head, so just continue to sit in silence as he speaks.

"I figured I would confess my feelings. However, it didn't happen because we weren't alone." He steps back.

I'm finally able to exhale the breath I was holding in. "Reece, I'm sorry you had a bad day," I respond, walking over to him. I avoid getting too close due to his frustration. I grab both his wrists. "What can I do to help?"

He lifts his right hand and places it on my face. His eyes begin to water.

"Reece…"

"The person I'm talking about is you. I think I'm falling in love with you, Cameron."

My heart starts racing in my chest. The words *falling in love with you, Cameron"* play over and over in my head. *This can't be happening. We've become such great friends. I mean yeah, we've spent a lot of time together connecting, but how could he like me in that way?*

He looks at me as if waiting for me to say something. I'm at a complete loss for words. I open my mouth, but nothing comes out. I release his wrists and begin walking towards the front door. As soon as I open it, he forces it closed. I see the frustration on his face.

"I'm not finished."

I try pulling the door open, but it won't budge. I continue pulling with all my strength. He finally removes his hand, and I'm able to bolt outside. The cool night breeze hits me in the face. I race to my car. Once inside, I slam my head against the steering wheel and begin pounding it with my fists. I start to cry and scream at the same time. I place a hand on my chest as the tears begin to flow. The door opens, and Reece pulls me out by my sleeve. He kicks the door closed and drags me to the front of the car. I push him off.

"I have more to say." He continues to drag me back towards the house. He kicks open the door and hurls me in. I fumble, but manage to keep my balance. The door is still open, so I'm gonna try and get out. I manage to push past him, but he pulls the back of my collar until we're in the center of the room. He holds up a palm, signaling me to stop. He walks over and slams the door.

The painting hanging near the window falls. I'm breathing heavily from our scuffle.

"I never dated guys," I say while trying to catch my breath.

"Neither have I," he says.

What? How is that possible? That day while hiking, he mentioned he was interested in a guy or girl didn't he?

"This doesn't make sense, you said…." He runs his left hand through his hair.

"You said I would find her and I said or him; I never said I've dated one. That was your assumption."

"But the club—"

"I found it online."

"On the dance floor, you took off your shirt like it was the usual."

"I had a lot to drink; I was nervous and drunk."

No, too much has happened to say these were just assumptions of my own.

"At the restaurant with the waiter—"

He groans in agitation, cutting me off. "It was conversation."

"Why did you kiss me?" That's one thing I know he can't make an excuse for.

"I was in the moment; you were staring at me and I thought you wanted to as well." At a loss for words, I take a seat while trying to control my breathing.

"How do you know?" I ask, looking up at him. "How do you know you like me?"

"When I'm with you, I feel brave, brave enough to face any fear," he says, walking towards me. "And I feel strong; strong enough to say no, but I also feel weak enough to be vulnerable."

As he gets closer, I see a tear roll down his cheek.

"I feel great about myself; I scream with excitement inside every time you're near."

Once I feel calm enough, I stand up. "Reece," I say softly as my voice begins to croak.

He turns around and places his hand over his face.

"Look at me."

He keeps his back to me. My eyes burn as tears start to flow.

"I'm sorry… but I'm unable to give you the response you want." I wait for him to say something, but all I get is the sound of him crying. After a few seconds, he spins around to face me.

He wipes his face clean. His eyes are red.

"I'm sorry," he says. "Sorry for loving you… sorry for caring for you… sorry for putting you before myself."

I turn towards the wall, unsure of how to respond.

"You have to figure out what you want," he sniffs. "It might take some time, but I know it doesn't include Riley."

Anger begins to rise inside of me. "I'm done with this," I respond turning back

He wipes his face once more. "Good… I'm done talking… Now get out."

He opens the door. I'm not sure what hurt most—him being upset with me or demanding that I leave.

43

HELLO EPIPHANY

My eyes are flooded with tears as I speed down the road. So much is happening too fast. When I moved out here, I was hoping to grow as a person. I figured somewhere new would bring more excitement to my life; I didn't expect so much confusion. You would think I'd be elated and over the moon since Riley confessed her feelings to me, but instead, I'm totally overwhelmed by anguish and sadness. Sadness from losing my best friend and a new friend. I wish I could just reset everything that has happened this week. Maybe then I could re-do every action.

I enter the freeway. There are so many slow-driving cars. I jump over to the next lane. A car behind me honks its horn. I honk back as it speeds past me. My phone starts ringing. I fumble around to grab it from my pocket, but drop it onto the floor. I let out a scream of frustration as I keep driving. I leave it lying on the floor; I'm not in the mood to talk. I just want to sleep the rest of the night away, forgetting all this pain I'm feeling. A car in front of me slows down. I swerve into the next lane, passing it up. My phone rings again. I let out another cry of aggravation and pound the steering wheel. Once I see the traffic ahead of me stopping, I begin to slow down my speed. Now we're at a standstill. I hear my phone ring again. I reach down to retrieve my phone and hear tires screeching from behind. I whip my head up in time to see a car with bright lights coming straight towards me. It smashes my vehicle from behind and I careen into the one in front of me. My head hits the steering wheel. It's the last thing I see before blacking out.

The sound of a monitor beeping fills my ears. I open my eyes. My vision is blurry. I touch the left side of my head due to the pain and pounding. There's a bandage covering my eyebrow. I scream in pain. Even my eyes seem to hurt from the light shining through the blinds, but then my vision begins to focus. The door opens and in comes a woman wearing a white coat. I watch as she reviews some documents attached to a clipboard. After a few moments of silence, she looks up to see me staring at her.

"Good afternoon. I'm Doctor Troy."

I continue to watch as she walks closer. She retrieves something from her coat pocket and points it towards my eye. Light comes out of the device and causes me to turn my head and groan.

She places it back inside her coat.

"Photophobia—it'll fade away," she says.

"What is that?"

My head begins to throb more.

"Light sensitivity."

I don't think I've experienced it before; why now?

"You've been in a coma for five days."

Five days? There's no way. I was just in a car accident last night. The sound of the monitor speeds up faster. My heart is now racing. How can it be five days later? "I understand how alarming this must be, but it's best to remain calm." How does she expect me to stay calm after something like this?

"I have to go," I say as I start removing the cover.

Before I get far, she puts a hand against my shoulder to keep me from getting up further.

"I'm afraid we'll have to keep you here for another day or two," she says.

"What time is it?" I ask.

"It's noon."

There is no way I'm staying here any longer.

"I need to make a call," I say.

She nods her head and steps into the hall. Once she leaves, I pull out the needle located in my right arm.

"Ouch!" I scream in pain. I cover my mouth as I continue to groan. I look around for my clothes, but can't find anything to change into. I walk into the restroom and lock the door. I look at myself in the mirror. *How can this be? Five days?* I notice the bandage covering my left eyebrow has a red stain. I peel it back to get a clear view and see fresh stitches.

I begin to feel lightheaded. I sit on the edge of the tub behind me. I place my hand on the left side of my head. The pain is becoming unbearable. I pull myself up with the door handle and step out into the hallway, leaning onto the wall.

"Sir, you shouldn't be out of bed," a nurse behind a desk says.

I continue walking down the hallway.

"Sir!" he says again.

I manage to reach the elevator and wait for it to arrive. I hear the same voice say, "He's down there." The doors open, and I step in. Before they close, I see the doctor standing there with an officer. I slide down and sit, waiting until I arrive on the first floor. The doors open, and I muster up enough strength to pick myself up. With blurry vision, I stumble as fast as I can towards the exit door. *Come on, Cameron, almost there.*

"Hey, stop!" someone behind me says.

I ignore them and continue to the door. Once outside, I shield my eyes. The sun is so bright.

I look around and see people staring at me in my hospital gown.

"Are you okay?" a woman to my left asks. She takes a step towards me as I go in the other direction. I look to the right to see a guy with two kids also staring at me.

"I don't think you should be standing," he says.

As best I can, I rush my way to the parking lot. My legs grow weak as I continue trying to go forward. I'm exhausted by the heat and the light, but I have to keep moving. But once I make it towards the end of the lot, I fall to the ground. I turn on my back and see Doctor Troy standing over me.

"I want to leave," I say in between heavy breaths. Then I see several pairs of feet running towards me before my vision fades.

HELLO NEW BEGINNING

I wake to find myself lying in a hospital bed again. My head is still throbbing. I lift myself up a little and look to my left. Leah, covered by a blanket, sleeping in the chair next to me.

How long have I been out? I touch the left side of my forehead. A bandage still covers the stitches.

My right arm is in pain. It could be from pulling out the IV or when I fell.

"Hey, you're up," Leah says softly. A weak smile appears on her face.

I watch as she gets up and walks over to me. She places her hand on my forehead.

"Leah, how long have I been asleep?"

I look towards the curtains, not seeing any daylight. She removes her hand and rubs my head. "You were in a coma for five days." At least today is the same day I woke up.

"What time is it?" I ask.

She looks at her phone.

"It's 7:00 PM"

I've been out for seven hours!

"Cam, what happened that night?"

Thoughts of the night Reece and I argued drift into my mind. I remember I left crying. I also remembered trying to grab my phone and…

"Someone hit me from behind," I say.

"What happened before the accident?" Her eyes begin to water. "I spoke to Reece; he said you were coming from his place."

He didn't tell her. If he didn't say anything, would it be appropriate if I did?

"We just had some things we needed to clear up," I say.

She sits next to me on the bed. "I didn't realize how much you were suffering. I blamed you for my situation, but didn't think about how uncomfortable it made you." Tears begin to stream down her cheeks.

I embrace her in a hug.

"Cameron, I told him; I told Anthony." I pull back.

"You're right; he deserves to know."

"How did he react?" I ask nervously.

"The first thing he said was, 'I'm going to be a dad.' When I heard those words, I just felt a weight lift off my shoulders." I wipe away her tears.

"And my mom's also happy; she can't wait to meet her grandchild." Leah just looks at me for a second. "Thank you for being there, Cam. Even when I was a jerk, you never left. I'm so sorry."

I embrace her in another hug.

The door opens behind me. I turn to see Reece standing there with massive smile and a bag in his hand. The last time I saw him, his face was covered in tears. It's nice to see him looking like this. I return the smile. He walks over to the bed and hugs me.

"I'm glad you're awake."

He continues to embrace me for a while longer. I hear Leah take a few steps before she appears in my view.

"I'll be back. It seems like you two need to talk," she says, shutting the door behind her.

Reece takes a seat in the same chair Leah had been sitting in.

"How do you feel?" he asks.

I still have a migraine, but I'm glad he's here.

"Better," I reply. I look at the shopping bag he brought in with bright blue tissue paper sprouting out of it. I wonder what he got. He lifts the bag and hands it towards me. I look inside to see a brown teddy bear. It's dressed in blue overalls. I can't contain my laughter. "I thought it might make you happy." I look to see him grinning.

"Thank you," I say, still looking at the bear.

He walks over and looks out the window. "I was scared," he says with a crack in his voice.

"I didn't want my last moment with you to be a fight. I owe you an apology," he says, wiping his face. "I'm sorry for how I reacted. I had no right to do what I did or say the things I said to you."

I should be the one who apologizes to him.

"You did nothing wrong," I say, wiping away the tear that streamed down my cheek. "I'm sorry for acting the way I did." I start sliding towards the edge of the bed. "Can you forgive me?"

He spins around and stares. I lower my head. I hurt him that night; I was too ashamed and afraid to face him. He takes a few steps until he's standing in front of me. He lifts my head until our eyes meet. He nods his head yes.

"I was jealous," he says. "I didn't understand why you were so head over heels for her, but there's no excuse for my behavior, I'll do better in controlling my feelings." He walks back towards the window.

Riley has the qualities of what I'm looking for in a person. She's kind, funny, intelligent, adventurous. He's also those things… as well as patient, brave, and strong. *Could it be that Reece also has the qualities I want?* I was so focused on Riley that I never considered what else had been in front of me all this time. Even when we first really hung out and Leah and Anthony were making trouble, he was great. He never judged my friends or me. He consoled me when I was sad. He also gave me a shoulder to cry on. That isn't something that comes by often. *So why am I so afraid of a different kind of ending?* Sure, Riley is a match for me. However, why can't it be possible to have more than one?

I pull myself up out of bed.

"Reece," I say softly.

He turns around and rushes over to me. He grabs both of my shoulders.

"Cam, you shouldn't be out of bed," he says frantically.

I hold onto his arms and look into those beautiful eyes of his. My eyes begin to water as I remember the moments he and I have shared. The one that stands out the most to me was the picnic. That was the day we got to know more of each other. He calls my name. But instead of responding with words, I wrap my arms around him.

"This is new to me," I say and let him rub my head.

"What do you mean?'

I release him and slowly take a seat on the bed. My legs are about to give out, but I have to say something.

"When I'm with you I feel brave enough to face any fear. I feel strong enough to say no.

And I'm weak enough to be vulnerable."

Tears begin streaming down his face. He steps back and sits in the chair, unable to speak.

"I want you in my life," I continue.

He steps forward.

"Are you saying what I think you're saying?" he asks.

I nod my head yes.

ACKNOWLEDGMENTS

To my editors David and Richard, thank you both for being kind and patient with me. I'm lucky enough to have found creative critique partners. To my illustrator Diego, thank you for your time, patience, and effort in creating a beautiful book cover. To my readers, thank you for giving my debut novel a chance.

ABOUT THE AUTHOR

C.D. Sterling is a Texas native who enjoys hiking, road trips, frozen yogurt, music, and learning new languages. He also enjoys some foreign films and shows. His passion for writing started at fourteen, with a painting in art class. He reads a variety of genres. For Love I Will is his debut novel.

9 7 9 8 9 9 1 1 3 6 6 1 7